Praise for *Love in C[...]*

"Fans of Sarah Dunn, Elisabeth Egan, and Isabel Gillies will relate to the multifaceted lives of Krien's characters, brilliantly rendered in her vivid voice."
—*Booklist*

"German novelist and award-winning short story author Krien (*Someday We'll Tell Each Other Everything*) has produced a sensitive, intricate study of the connected stories of her characters, who seek a shield against the deep loneliness caused by unwanted solitude or by being with the wrong person. Readers will find something relatable in one or more of the lives of these women."
—*Library Journal*

"Witty and candid, *Love in Case of Emergency* deftly examines the world of relationships, and the challenges, ambitions, and failures of the women who take part in them."
—*Shelf Awareness*

"[*Love in Case of Emergency*] is hopeful but never sentimental about how love might be parsed, and Krien is unfailingly impressive in her depiction of the lives of these five very different women."
—*Irish Times*

"In spite of its serious subject, *Love in Case of Emergency* is a novel that will make your heart jump for joy."
—Gérard Otremba, *Sounds and Books*

Love
in
Case
of
Emergency

Also by Daniela Krien in English translation

Someday We'll Tell Each Other Everything

Love
in
Case
of
Emergency

a novel

Daniela Krien

Translated from the German by Jamie Bulloch

 HarperVia

An Imprint of HarperCollinsPublishers

LOVE IN CASE OF EMERGENCY. Copyright © 2019 by Diogenes Verlag AG. All rights reserved. Printed in the United States of America. No part of this book may be used or reproduced in any manner whatsoever without written permission except in the case of brief quotations embodied in critical articles and reviews. For information, address HarperCollins Publishers, 195 Broadway, New York, NY 10007.

HarperCollins books may be purchased for educational, business, or sales promotional use. For information, please email the Special Markets Department at SPsales@harpercollins.com.

English translation copyright © 2021 by Jamie Bulloch.

Originally published as *Die Liebe im Ernstfall* by Diogenes Verlag AG, Zurich, in 2019.

FIRST HARPERCOLLINS PAPERBACK EDITION PUBLISHED IN 2022

Designed by SBI Book Arts, LLC

Library of Congress Cataloging-in-Publication Data is available upon request.

ISBN 978-0-06-300601-0

22 23 24 25 26 LSC 10 9 8 7 6 5 4 3 2 1

Contents

PART ONE

Paula

The day Paula realizes she's happy is a Sunday in March. It's raining. It started during the night and hasn't stopped since. When Paula wakes around half past eight the rain is pounding against her sloping bedroom window. She turns onto her side and pulls the duvet up to her chin. She didn't wake up once last night and can't remember having dreamed, either.

Her mouth is dry and a slight pressure inside her skull reminds Paula of yesterday evening. Wenzel cooked dinner and opened a bottle of French red to go with it. Afterward they sat on the sofa and listened to music—Mahler's *Song of the Earth*, Beethoven's last piano sonata, Schubert's *Lieder*, Brahms, and Mendelssohn. They searched YouTube for different artists, compared their performances, and squealed in childish delight whenever their opinions concurred.

Paula could have stayed at his place, spent the night with him, but she claimed to have left her medicine at home. The hydrocortisone was in her handbag. In fact what she didn't have were her toothbrush and facial cleanser. Wenzel would have said these weren't important and would have persuaded her to stay.

She got into a taxi at around two in the morning. Wenzel stood outside until the car turned the corner.

✳

She reaches for the bottle of water beside her bed, takes a glug, then switches on her phone and reads his message: **Morning, darling. Thinking of you, as always.** A text every morning and evening. For the past ten months, without exception.

Leni likes Wenzel, too, and Wenzel likes Leni.

When they first met, he impressed her with a very rapid sketch of her face. The resemblance was striking, and Leni wanted him to do more so she could show off at school.

✳

Paula checks the time. Nine hours until Leni comes back. Either she'll chuck her things on the floor, mumble a hello, and withdraw to her room or, without pausing for breath, give a detailed report of the weekend, including photographs of her half sister and a rhapsody about Filippa's cooking.

As Paula replies to Wenzel's morning greeting, she wishes she were with him.

Her desire for him is always at its greatest in the morning. When she goes to the kitchen to put on the coffee, she writes him an unambiguous text.

Since Paula has had Wenzel in her life she hasn't missed Leni so much on the weekends. And what could she do, anyway? Leni isn't a child anymore. In the mornings she practices a variety of smiles in front of the mirror, she makes rips in her trousers, wears shirts that appear to slide casually off the shoulder, uses lip gloss, and sends cryptic messages to the 7b class chat, consisting chiefly of emojis and abbreviations. Sometimes she'll talk nonstop, only to lapse into an aggressive silence shortly afterward. She copes with her nightmares on her own and Paula hasn't seen her daughter naked for a while now. Not even that morning when Leni asked if it's possible to have saggy breasts when you're thirteen. She said she'd looked at hers and decided that they were *that* shape. With her right hand she drew a ridiculously exaggerated outline in the air, keeping her left hand pressed to her chest. Before Paula could reply, Leni was berating her mother for having passed on only her worst features: freckles, pale skin, red hair, knobbly knees, and a total ineptitude in physics and chemistry.

Pointing out that genetic inheritance was pure chance, not a conscious decision, Paula was about to stroke her daughter's hair, but Leni pulled away and dashed out, slamming the door behind her. She came back soon after and threw herself into Paula's arms, as if stocking up for the next stage of detachment.

*

It's still raining. Paula squeezes some oranges and froths milk for her coffee. A vase of tulips is on the table.

One year ago the length of the day that lay ahead would have sent her into a panic. She would have started cleaning or doing the washing, gone for a jog or to see a film, or called Judith and gone with her to see the horse. *What* she did wasn't important, all that mattered was that she did *something*. Otherwise the demons would have surfaced to haunt her.

* * *

After she separated from Ludger, she often wondered what had marked the beginning of the end. When had things gotten out of control?

Johanna's death had been a watershed. But as time passed, Paula began to attribute the failure of their relationship to other, earlier events, going further and further back until there was no more *back*.

It all began with a party.

When the organic shop in Südvorstadt celebrated its opening, Paula and Judith were passing by chance. They'd been at the lake, sunbathing in the nude, rubbing sun lotion into each other, eating ice cream and attracting plenty of looks. Satisfied with themselves and the impression they'd made, they cycled past the wildlife park, through the floodplain forest, and back into town where it was still hot and sticky.

From a distance they noticed the balloons, the planters full of flowers, and the crowd of people outside the shop. Eager for a cold drink, they stopped.

Ludger was standing near the door when they entered. Paula noticed him right away. Later he said that he'd caught sight of her out of the corner of his eye, too, and his gaze had followed her. Paula was wearing a moss-colored strapless dress and a sunhat, from beneath which her red locks flowed.

Outside the sun was scorching, the odor of exhaust fumes and lime blossom hung in the streets, and every breath of wind blew the sticky-sweet concoction into the shop. Ludger was wearing a linen shirt. His hair was blond, his eyes blue. He wasn't the conqueror type.

The two of them left the party shortly afterward, chatting as they wheeled their bikes along the street.

Ludger kept looking at her, but he did not hold her gaze. When he spoke at any length, he stopped.

Like Paula, he tried to stay in the shade.

By the riverbank he casually stroked her arm.

On a park bench in the evening light she kissed him.

✳

In the first few weeks they saw each other every day.

Their meetings would begin by an oak tree in Clara-Park. Paula, who arrived everywhere too early, saw him turn onto the path on his racing bike and waved at him immediately. Every encounter began with slight embarrassment, though this dissipated after the first kiss.

From the tree they wandered through the parks and the neighboring parts of town. Paula loved the way he cocked his head to one side and beamed whenever he saw her. She also liked his deep voice and soft way of speaking. His boundless energy was infectious, and she was impressed by his knowledge of sustainable building and self-sufficiency as well as of flora and fauna.

Ludger often came to see her in the bookshop.

Sometimes she glimpsed his head first, as he rode the escalator up to the fiction section. Sometimes he surprised her in the middle of sorting books or placing orders. He would discreetly caress her hand or arm and she would turn to him, feeling a secret thrill that her female colleagues could see how handsome he was.

Their nights together were spent at his place. Only once did he sleep at her apartment, which at the time she was sharing with Judith. The three of them had spent the evening together over pizza and red wine. Time and again Ludger managed to bring the conversation back to his area of expertise: the environmental footprint that each person left and how to keep it as small as possible. He kept interrupting Judith to enlarge upon a topic or correct an inaccurate statement.

Noticing her friend's jiggling foot and the tense expression on her face, Paula got the message.

The next day Judith came into her room carrying a pile of medical books. She explained to Paula that she needed some peace in the apartment so close to her final exams and it would help if Ludger didn't come again for the time being.

✳

At night they lay closely entwined in bed.

Their hands or feet were always touching. Paula would stroke his back, counting the chimes from the church bell tower, and if there was enough time before they had to get up she would put her hands between his legs.

She was not worried about how they made love, or how Ludger said *that* to refer to everything they did in bed. Do you like *that*? Do you want to do *that*? Nor was she surprised that he recoiled when she first explored the unmentionable parts of his body with her tongue. In the end he allowed it. He lay there perfectly still, arms crossed over his face.

Afterward they were outstretched.

Ludger talked about his parents' death. When he told her how they'd been crushed by a lorry at the back of a traffic jam, his voice became stilted. He'd been awarded his architecture diploma only a few days earlier.

Paula kissed his shoulders and neck, and he laid his head on her chest.

*

A few months after they met, Ludger asked her to pop by his office. He sounded excited, but he didn't want to tell her why on the phone. When Paula turned up at Brinkmann & Krohn, the Brinkmann brothers swiveled around in their chairs simultaneously and grinned. Bowing his head, Ludger took Paula by the hand and led her into the conference room.

On the table were the plans for an apartment. It was a loft with twelve-foot-high ceilings and 3,000 square feet of living space. Without pausing for breath, he explained where platforms would give the space structure, where the stairs would lead up to an open gallery, and how the accommodation could work without individual rooms or even partition walls. Carried away by his own enthusiasm, at the end he said almost casually: *That's where we're going to live.*

Paula said nothing. It took a few moments to sink in.

She recalled how often he mentioned that the church opposite his apartment depressed him. Ludger didn't want to be reminded on a daily basis of the houses of worship that the *Christian folk*, as he called them, had erected for their god.

What do you think? he said. *Are you pleased?*

The following day they cycled to the viewing, meeting beforehand at the oak tree in the park. With hats, scarves, and gloves they made their way to one of those parts of town Paula rarely visited, but which Ludger predicted was rapidly up and coming. The loft was in a building on a tree-lined cobbled street, looked out onto the canal, and was as large as a station concourse. Not only were there no churches nearby, there wasn't much else, either. The masonry was unrendered, it was cold inside, and her first instinct was to get away from there as quickly as possible.

Ludger laid the plans out on the floor. He paced out the hall, checked the walls and windows, and then launched into his spiel. Paula could already visualize the kitchen area on its wooden platform, feel the floorboards beneath her feet, climb the stairs to the sleeping area, and, leaning against the gallery banisters, gaze out over the entire space.

*

Parting from Judith was difficult.

They had shared an apartment for five happy years. Paula was closer to her than to anyone else. As babies they'd been pushed side by side by their mothers in almost identical prams, they had the same crib, went to the same kindergarten, same elementary school. They were confirmed together, got their periods in the same month of the same year, and both left Naumburg when they were eighteen. Judith went to Leipzig to study medicine, Paula to Regensburg for a bookselling apprenticeship.

When the time came to move, a very aloof Judith merely got in the way. She listened in silence as everyone heaped praise on the new apartment, and she said good-bye to Paula before the final box had been loaded onto the moving van.

*

During the first few months they lived together, there was only one thing on Ludger's mind: a renovation project in the city center. It was a seventeenth-century house. Despite the renovation, the dampness and mold kept coming back. The architects who were commissioned first had been taken off the job; their new fees were far higher than the original estimates. Ludger saw his opportunity and made an offer that nobody could undercut. It was so economical that people became suspicious, and the solution sounded too good to be true.

The inventor of the method, the restorer Henning Grosse-schmidt, had successfully tried out the *tempering* principle of heat distribution in many palaces and museums. Ludger was his pupil and had attended several of Grosseschmidt's seminars.

Instead of using normal radiators, heating pipes were embedded in the external walls beneath the plaster, and the even levels of heat these produced solved the problem of dampness and mold. The temperature and air quality inside the room improved, while the energy expenditure and maintenance were low.

Even over dinner Ludger would unfold plans on the table and explain to Paula how far into the walls the pipes were embedded, what material they were made from, and in which buildings the method had already been successfully applied. On his lips, the word *tempering* sounded almost reverential. Not once did the planning of their forthcoming wedding spark a similar level of enthusiasm.

Ludger refused to have a church wedding and Paula acquiesced. It felt right to achieve harmony by way of agreement. Most of the wedding guests were from her side too. Ludger invited the Brinkmann brothers and their wives, as well as the team who had helped them move. None of his relatives were invited. His contacts were limited to colleagues, clients, and tradesmen.

Paula took charge of planning the meal, as well as the choice of drinks, the design of the invitation, and the decoration of their apartment. Ludger only wanted a say in the music.

They sat there half the night, Ludger going through his jazz records for the best tracks, smoking, occasionally humming along. When Paula started dancing after her second glass of wine, he watched her with the embarrassment she was now familiar with.

Head bowed, shoulders hunched, beer bottle up to his lips, he sat there, his eyes following her.

When Paula fell into his lap, he put the beer aside, wrapped his arms around her waist, and kissed her. Seconds later he pushed her away and stood up. His body tensed, his gaze wandered the room, and excitedly he announced that tempering would be the best solution for this apartment, too.

*

Nobody was exactly how you wanted them to be.

Paula hoped that time would close the gap between wishing and reality.

* * *

She's still in her nightie when she steps out onto the balcony after breakfast and gazes down at the garden. It's Paula's fifth apartment in this city; at last she feels at home.

Crocuses and snowdrops are blooming in the communal garden, which is divided off from the neighboring plots by high stone walls. Beneath Paula and Leni are a family with two small children, and an elderly couple have the apartment on the ground floor. For the most part they live in a state of peaceful coexistence. It's only the garden that leads to the occasional dispute. The elderly couple's desire for order clashes with the random and rarely successful spontaneous attempts at planting by the family on the first floor. But overall a mutual respect prevails and once a year they all have a summer party.

Paula wanders slowly down the length of the balcony that extends across the width of three rooms, each of which has a door opening onto it. The rain gradually subsides, and still there's no answer from Wenzel. Maybe he's working in his studio, maybe he hasn't read her message, or maybe he's on his way to her. She has no doubt that he will come.

She runs her hands along the wooden railing, focusing on the movements of her arms, her hands, then on her breathing and realizing that she has to strain to feel her body. It doesn't insinuate itself through pain, inflexibility, or excessive torpor. She no longer takes for granted what is seemingly self-evident.

While she was married to Ludger the future appeared hazy; after Johanna's death, the past looked crystal clear. Back in the present she hears the doorbell and hurries to her front door.

Wenzel has some flowers he nabbed on his way through the park. Later they will be put in tiny vases in Paula's apartment.

He's shaved his thinning hair. Wenzel is the first man she hasn't tried to mold. The first who sometimes focuses solely on her desire. The first she hasn't introduced to her parents.

She takes his hand and leads him to the bedroom.

He slowly undresses her, instructs her to lie on her tummy, and runs his fingertips firmly from her neck to her thighs, then pushes these apart, and she's briefly reminded of what she keeps bottled up. Then she tells him about the men. Tells him how far she went, what she let them do, just so she could feel a different pain. A pain that dominated the grief rampaging inside her like an unleashed demon. With tears in her eyes she tells him what she was ashamed of, what she enjoyed *despite* the shame, and how submission allowed her to forget the death of her child for a few hours. And when she finishes talking, he kisses her and his lips follow the path taken by his fingertips.

On the morning of Paula and Ludger's wedding they were woken by a noise. A window had been left open and a bird had flown in during the night. Panic-stricken, it was flapping around the lamps and furniture. It flew against a windowpane and crashed to the floor, then made another attempt but again missed the opening.

Paula leaped out of bed and opened all the windows. Her heart was racing. She winced every time the bird collided with the glass. Ludger helped her and together they shooed it around the huge room. But to no avail. The bird couldn't find its way out. It was still early; a pink sky heralded daybreak. The bird lay on the floor and they decided to wait.

Back in bed, Ludger snuggled up close. He put an arm around her and nuzzled into her hair. His fingertips caressed her belly. When a shudder ran through her body, he stopped, then fell asleep soon afterward.

Paula listened to the flapping of wings and the bird's short, shrill cries as her fingers moved between her open legs. She had carefully shuffled out of Ludger's embrace. She lay on her tummy and pressed her face into the pillow.

When the alarm went off, she woke with a start. She got up at once and searched the room. The bird had disappeared.

*

Paula returned pleasantly exhausted from their honeymoon, which they spent hiking in the Vosges. Starting in Sainte-Odile, they walked to Kaysersberg via the Col du Kreuzweg and then headed south to the nature reserve, in ever-changing weather and negotiating, in Paula's view, endless perilous ascents and descents. Sometimes they walked for hours in silence, one in front of the other, because the paths were narrow and talking wasted too much energy. Then they were side by side again, imagining their future together.

For long stretches they wouldn't meet another soul. They picnicked on sun-warmed rocks, in ruined castles and old war fortifications.

As soon as they took a break, Ludger would unpack the maps. He had several in different scales, and he kept pointing out to Paula exactly where they were. As they ate bread, cheese, and apples he explained the route they would be taking over the next few hours. There was no limit to his enthusiasm for the precision of the hiking maps, which showed even the tiniest path.

They spent the nights in *fermes auberges*, sharing dormitories with other hikers. Only on the first and last nights of their ten-day trip did they sleep in hotels, with their own bathroom and a comfy double bed, and those were the only two nights they made love. Ludger had a habit of curling up afterward and nestling his head on Paula's chest. This was how he liked going to sleep. Whenever Paula, who couldn't sleep in that position, carefully turned away, he followed her. Even in the deepest sleep he would snuggle back up to her the moment their bodies lost contact. Paula would then get up and move round to the other side of the bed. All the same, she liked this physical confirmation of his love.

∗

On the first day back at work after the honeymoon, Paula's colleagues greeted her by her new name: Paula Krohn. And when Marion, who also worked in the fiction department, called out at the end of the day, *Paula, your husband's here!*, she stood up and smiled.

It was a moment she would cherish, even in hindsight.

In jeans and a T-shirt, Ludger stood beside the table with the new releases and waved to her. She could not have said why this made her feel proud.

∗

The hormonal fog lifted.

Paula spent many evenings alone in the loft. If she opened the window that looked onto the canal, the brackish odor of the filthy water wafted in, but if she closed the window, it went eerily quiet. Her own voice echoed around the cavernous space. There were no separate rooms, just a cube in the middle that housed the bathroom.

Every evening she waited for Ludger to come home. The tempering job took up his time like no other project and he often got back late. While she waited, she cooked, read, made telephone calls, or stood by the window, never forgetting that everything she was doing was merely killing time. The tension only ended when she heard his key in the lock and Paula wondered whether it was really just down to the apartment and its emptiness.

Birds kept straying into the loft. Not all of them found their way out. One day she found a pigeon with a broken wing sitting on the floor beside the dining table. A dead sparrow lay beneath the window through which it had flown.

From then on the windows remained closed.

*

Every Sunday they had breakfast at Café Telegraph.

Ludger would read the *F.A.Z.* and the *Neue Zürcher Zeitung*, Paula *Der Spiegel* and *Die Zeit*.

They rode the cycle paths along the Saale and the Mulde, visited exhibitions, went to the cinema and bickered about which film to see. Ludger preferred documentaries; Paula, biopics of artists. Ludger said critically that Paula wouldn't have lasted a single day in the life of Georg Trakl, or a week with

Camille Claudel. She, on the other hand, complained that he took everything too seriously. He had no sense of humor, no levity, she said, while he retorted that it was levity and carelessness that was causing the world to go to ruin.

They argued about things that neither would have imagined one could argue about. When they went cycling, he rode quicker than she did. He didn't look back to see where she was. He raced across lights that were turning red and kept going, while Paula waited for them to turn green again. He also decided where they would go. He always knew the best route from any point in the city to any other. Resistance would be broken by a glance at the map that he always had on hand.

Sometimes she would deliberately fall behind and go her own way. She knew how much this annoyed him and she knew that the reconciliation would occasionally occur in bed.

When Ludger was angry, he did not put a check on his physical strength. The sex was freer than usual. And those were the nights that gave Paula hope. On other nights she would lie awake, wriggle from his embrace, and not know what to do with her desire.

꘏

The first decision that Paula forced through was to move out of the loft.

It wasn't a sensible place to live. Rental prices were increasing and Ludger was facing a crisis.

Despite his success, there hadn't been any more tempering

commissions. His goal had seemed so close. Ludger had been sure that Brinkmann & Krohn were on the verge of gaining the reputation as the best architectural practice for sustainable building. He had turned down other, more lucrative contracts and quarreled with the Brinkmann brothers.

At that time the child inside her belly was about three inches long. It could stick its thumb in its mouth and hold the umbilical cord between its fingers, and it moved animatedly.

The ultrasound image lay on the table between them. Paula was crying. She'd been talking, begging him. *Walls and rooms!*, Ludger had parroted back at her, shaking his head. Their bed was big enough for three, he claimed, and the loft was ideal for a small child. It could ride a bike, trampoline, swing—what more did she want?

When Paula got up from the table, she wiped the tears from her face, grabbed the ultrasound image, and put it in her pocket.

Over the months that followed she rode her Gazelle bike the length and breadth of the city. She spoke to estate agents and private landlords, viewed endless apartments, and narrowed down the list that she presented to Ludger in the evenings.

It then turned out that the apartments were in areas of the city that were absolute no-nos for Ludger: streets without trees and therefore unacceptable; in states of redevelopment he couldn't live with; neighbors he didn't like the sound of. He refused to live next door to lawyers, accountants, or estate agents. He hated their SUVs, from which they looked down on everyone else, violated the traffic laws, and double-parked. He dreaded their status symbols, their felling of trees to create new parking places, their complete ignorance of real life.

One day, as they were standing on the balcony of a partially renovated four-room apartment, looking out at the southern end of the floodplain forest, Ludger finally relented, but Paula didn't feel any happiness. The damp, musty smell of the ramsons made her feel sick. She leaned against the balcony railings and closed her eyes.

The apartment was at the rear of the development. There was no street noise, no rattling of trams, just the green crowns of the trees and birdsong. It was ten minutes to the center of town by bike and both their workplaces were just as quick to get to. The stairwell was full of bicycles and no matter which window you looked out of you couldn't see a single car. It was perfect.

On the day of their move Paula could only watch and give instructions. The baby was due in four weeks. Her legs ached, and her shoes pinched her swollen feet. All she wanted to do was to withdraw to the refuge of her shell like a snail.

At the end of that day, however, the only thing in its place, amid all the chaos of boxes, suitcases, and furniture parts, was the bed. And when she finally lay down, Paula thought of those nights she'd spent in it sleeplessly, and of the child in her belly who was still without a name.

The baby was two weeks premature and it arrived in that same bed. The home birth had been Ludger's idea. She didn't tell Judith, who was now a junior doctor in Hanover. Paula knew her friend's opinion. *Medieval,* she would have said, *totally nutty.*

She had calmed her own anxieties with the certainty that

a doctor could be there within minutes if necessary. Her colleagues had encouraged her to have the baby at home too. Stories went around about drug-resistant germs. A hospital was no safer place than one's own bed.

Now she kneeled beside the bed and looked up. A bare bulb hung from a cable. Lamps still needed to be connected and shelves put up. It had been twenty minutes since her phone call. *Take a taxi*, she'd said without much hope. But, as expected, Ludger came home by bike. She heard his key in the lock, his footsteps in the hallway, the sound of the bag tossed aside and then—nothing more. She breathed through a contraction, her focus now restricted to her back and womb.

For the next nine hours he kept going out and coming back in. Kneeled beside her, lay next to her, held her hand, and wiped sweat from her brow.

Hairband! she cried. *Music off!* she ordered and *Shut the window!* When the midwife finally allowed her to push, she had no strength left to talk.

But how quickly the details faded, how quickly the pain was forgotten. The midwife laid the baby on Paula's tummy, and when Paula saw that it was a girl she sank back into her pillow with a smile. Ludger cut the umbilical cord and soon afterward Leni Antonia Krohn was suckling at Paula's breast.

*

Ludger stayed at home for three weeks.

During this time he, she, and Leni were the whole world.

Even when the baby fed, he lay beside them. All the necessary trips out were completed as quickly as possible. The three of them were like a force field that lost its energy the moment one of them left the closed circle.

When she came for her final visit, the midwife remarked that she'd rarely worked with a family where everything ran so smoothly.

On their last day together they got up at dawn. Paula would have liked to stay in bed, having fed Leni every couple of hours during the night. She felt so exhausted that even going to the loo felt like too much effort.

The park was deserted. An early mist hung above the grass. There was an autumnal chill to the air. When they got to the oak tree where they'd always met, Ludger took off his rucksack, unpacked the pickax and spade, and started digging the hole. When the pick hit a root, it rebounded, almost hitting his head. He looked for another spot.

Leni had begun to cry. She lay in the pram, wrapped up warmly. Her arms were flailing and her bawling tore through the silence. Paula pushed the pram back and forth. A bicycle shot past. Soon the paths would be filled with cyclists, joggers, and dog owners. She slowly moved a few feet away from Ludger, acting as if they weren't together, as if she were just another passerby.

After about ten minutes, Ludger had dug a hole a foot deep. He reached into the rucksack and from a plastic bag took the placenta that was thawing. He held it in both hands for a while before placing it in the hole. Then he stretched out his arm to Paula.

His hand was wet and Paula noticed a sweet taste in her mouth.

Leni was still crying when Ludger had filled the hole. Paula turned around and briskly pushed the pram across the grass to the park. She only looked back once. A large dog was bounding purposefully to where the fresh earth stood proud of the green grass.

But before it reached the spot where they'd buried the placenta she turned away.

*

Everything was different now that she was alone with the child.

The rhythm of her day followed the infant's feeding and sleeping needs. Paula's body seemed alien to her. The breasts belonged to Leni, the limbs were heavy, the hair lifeless, and her belly took ages to return to its old shape.

When Ludger came home, he had eyes only for his daughter. If Paula was carrying the baby in her arms, he would reach out and grab Leni without asking. *Papa was at the construction site*, he would say, or *Papa's just got a new contract*. Then he would explain to Leni why low-energy houses were prone to mold, the advantages of clay panels, how he was trying to persuade his client of the benefits of tempering, and which grasses and herbs were suitable for a green roof.

In the evening he would potter around the apartment. Whatever he touched became beautiful. The illuminated shelves he designed for the storage room, the coat stand in the hallway, the extravagant lamps—everything was perfect in its imperfections.

Whenever he finished something, he would call Paula. She would come and praise him, and his hand would feel for hers.

Only later, in bed, with Leni lying between them and Ludger gazing at her in adoration, did Paula feel uneasy. The tenderness in his eyes was for their child alone. Every tiny sound she made delighted him.

She was ashamed at what she felt. But his emotion disgusted her.

*

As often as she could she met up with Judith again, who was back in Leipzig having started her specialist training.

Paula enjoyed these hours with Judith, when she was able to be witty, ironic, and confident. But the more time she spent with her, the harder she found it to readjust when she got home. And it became ever more difficult to hide the truth from her friend.

She didn't mention the nights when she woke up because her heart was beating too quickly. Nor the times when she felt everything was wrong, like a mistake that couldn't be rectified. Nor that Ludger and she hadn't made love in months. Before the birth it was the baby in her belly; after the birth the baby in the bed. A fleeting kiss in the mornings, a brief hug in the evenings. And nothing in between.

In those weeks Ludger often told her how happy he was. Paula got the impression she was paying the price for that happiness. As if he were living off her. The more energy he possessed, the weaker she felt. The more obsessively he forged his plans, the less motivated she became.

This was the period when he grew a beard, when he stopped eating meat and killing insects. When he installed a water filter and bought a grain flaker. When he began donating a significant proportion of his monthly salary to animal welfare and human rights organizations and switched his account to an ethical bank. His argument for all this was as simple as it was true: doing the right thing couldn't be wrong.

He spent many evenings thinking aloud about how they ought to live. About how they could further reduce their ecological impact. Paula sat at the table with him. A silent listener, giving the occasional nod.

At the same time his despondency toward the world and humanity grew. He wouldn't go into a café without earplugs as he couldn't bear to hear scraps of other people's private lives, being forced to participate in the lives of strangers. Paula could see his disgust from the tension in his face.

Essentially she shared his views. She had always admired Ludger's moral integrity and his willingness to practice self-denial. Unlike most people, he stood up for what he believed in and accepted the downsides. She understood his sensitivity, too. And like him, she wanted Leni to grow up in a better world. Wasn't this harmony of views the love Ludger spoke of?

But none of it had anything to do with her *personally*. With her—Paula.

✳ ✳ ✳

Paula, he whispers, stroking her hair from her tearstained face.

Wenzel understands. He seems to understand everything. He doesn't despise her, he doesn't judge, he doesn't even frown.

Before she first had sex with him she went to the doctor. She was certain she was ill. Paula had slept with fifteen men within the space of a year. According to the infidelity website, they were all married. Paula knew their first names and their ages, but nothing more. When they said they were healthy, she'd believed them.

The men hadn't wanted to know anything either.

By the time the results came back she'd known Wenzel for eight weeks. They'd gone to listen to a Brahms symphony and a Rachmaninov piano concerto, had been to the theater, taken long walks, and kissed on benches in the park. In the past she'd started and finished a relationship in eight weeks. But Wenzel hadn't even seen her naked.

To begin with she worried he would run off the moment he realized how damaged she was. But when he kept appearing punctually at the appointed meeting places, her anxiety gradually abated.

Standing by the desk at the doctor's office, Paula tried in vain to gauge the results from the face of the receptionist. The woman's eyes scanned a sheet of paper; her expression gave nothing away. She answered the telephone when it rang, scheduled an appointment, then glanced at the sheet of paper again. *Everything's fine, Frau Krohn,* she said without looking up.

Paula was riding her bicycle. The wind in her face was warm.

At the market she bought fish, tomatoes, peppers, cucumbers, radishes, lettuce, onions, garlic, fresh herbs, lemons, and saffron. Her panniers full, she stopped at the wine shop, tried a Grauburgunder, a Weissburgunder, and a Sauvignon Blanc, enjoyed the pleasant buzz from the alcohol and left the shop with a Silvaner from Franconia.

Back home she tied on an apron, put on some Chopin ballades, and started cooking.

It was the day the swifts suddenly appeared, as they did every year. Flying from south of the equator they arrived in the first week of May, tearing along the streets at breathtaking speed. Their shrill cries rang out in the evening and could even be heard through the closed windows.

Paula went into the living room and sat on the windowsill. For a few minutes the evening sun was reflected in one of the windows opposite. Her three-quarter profile was cast like a paper cutting onto the curtain that divided the room, the shadows of the swifts darting over it and away.

That night they made love for the first time. Wenzel didn't do anything Paula was unfamiliar with, and yet something about the sex was out of the ordinary. It was like a piece of complex music, with different, finer sounds emerging upon subsequent hearings, the beauty revealing itself in the quietest note and even in the pauses. And when she opened her eyes the next morning, Wenzel was still beside her.

* * *

When Ludger stopped calling her by her name, she deliberately started doing things he frowned upon.

One Sunday morning Paula took a fifteen-minute shower.

One Wednesday evening she threw a bruised apple in the bin in front of his eyes.

She bought clothes and shoes even though she had plenty of both. But she didn't hear her name again until one night she fried a steak.

Ludger had turned vegetarian only a few weeks earlier, but his decision was a topic of conversation every evening. He would cite statistics relating to global meat consumption, industrial livestock farming, and how much feed and water were used. His memory for figures was impressive and the inevitable consequence of this knowledge was self-denial.

When he arrived at the door with a *Hello, love!*, Paula took the steak from the pan and put it on her plate. She seasoned it with sea salt and pepper and helped herself to some salad. When she cut up the meat with a sharp knife, the juice seeped out. The steak was raw on the inside. A small trickle of blood made its way through the green salad leaves.

Paula's heart was in her mouth. No longer hungry, she briefly considered throwing the meat in the bin, but Ludger was already standing beside her.

What are you doing, love? he asked.

When she just looked at him in silence, he said *Paula!* and nothing else.

After she bought the car, he said hardly anything to her for weeks.

It was an unnecessarily large car: an old, black Volvo, almost twelve feet long.

He wandered around like a wounded soldier, stooped and downcast.

Paula wouldn't apologize. His silence tormented her, but when they finally spoke again, she defended her actions by saying that he wouldn't have agreed to it anyway. As she mopped the bathroom floor she said he was her *husband*, not her *master. Didn't she want someone to dominate her sometimes?* Ludger replied, and she laughed when she realized what he meant. A smile flickered across his lips, too, and she didn't let the opportunity go to waste. She kissed him, then bent over the washing machine. Ludger was still angry enough not to back off.

The peace didn't last long.

One Sunday afternoon the bell rang. Judith stormed in, went straight into the kitchen, and, without saying a word, laid photographs of a dark-brown quarter horse mare on the table. A few days earlier she had passed her endocrinology and diabetology exam. The horse was a present to herself.

With Leni in his arms, Ludger stared at the photographs while Judith raved about the horse's level of training, her rideability, suppleness, and docility when jumping. When she finished, he said with outright disgust that no ethically minded individual could ride or train animals, all of which caused unnecessary suffering.

Judith put her hands on her hips, glanced at Leni, and stuck out her chin defiantly. *If you want to avoid unnecessary suffering,* she said, *don't bring children into this world. For this child, like everyone else in the world, will experience suffering.*

She gathered up her photographs, put them in her bag, and looked at Paula. On any other day Paula might have taken her friend's side. On any other day she might have told Ludger not to impose his opinions on the entire world and not to pass judgment on anyone who lived differently.

Judith didn't visit for a long time after that.

She stopped calling and replied tersely and dismissively to Paula's messages. When Judith took over a GP's office from a friend of her mother's, Paula got the same invitation to the opening as all the other guests. With no personal message or any hint of their lifelong friendship.

Paula blamed Ludger for this.

She contemplated a separation.

But they didn't separate.

In the period that followed they became withdrawn. They turned down invitations and rarely had visitors. They had regular sex again. Their relationship worked in the inner circle of their love.

*

At the beginning of her second pregnancy apologies were given and promises made. Paula acknowledged that sometimes her actions were a protest, while Ludger confessed to trying too hard to educate her. These admissions made them feel that they'd cleared things up, and his affection confirmed her assumptions that their past problems wouldn't play a role in the future.

Hundreds of photographs were taken. Ludger and Leni in a dinghy on the lake, Paula and Leni sitting in the flowering ramsons, Leni and Ludger in front of a sloth in the zoo, all three of them lying on a meadow by the Mulde with daisy crowns in their hair.

As things were, they were good.

And as things were, they were fragile.

Paula only felt really calm when Ludger was with her. If he didn't come back when he said he would, she assumed the worst: he'd fallen off scaffolding on a building site, he'd had an accident on his bike or a brain aneurysm.

But nothing happened.

As far as the world outside was concerned, they were simply a lovely couple.

At a consultation evening for a forest school Leni was going to attend, Paula sensed the eyes of the other parents on them. They were all sitting in a large circle in a clearing, and she felt as if she were stepping out of her body and watching from outside: a confident, pregnant woman with a little redheaded girl in her lap and a thoughtful-looking, handsome man at her side, with his arm around her.

That evening they made love. Although she was pregnant, Paula drank a whole glass of red wine, and when Ludger joined her in bed, his hands immediately felt for her. All of a sudden his desire had returned. He kissed her hastily, but his fingers felt in vain for the usual warm dampness between her legs.

When it was over, they embraced tightly.

On other days everything seemed genuine and good. Such as when Ludger picked up Leni from the babysitter and brought her to the bookshop as a nice surprise for Paula. When they walked through the park to the playground, past the blooming jasmine and stopping at the ice cream van on Sachsenbrücke. When they got back to the area where they lived with the newly planted lime trees and the houses gleaming with fresh coats of paint. When Leni snuggled between them in the mornings and went back to sleep while the birds chirped outside. When they made plans and the future shone. When Ludger laid his hands on Paula's belly to feel the baby moving.

At times it seemed doubtful that this child would ever acquire a name. Ludger's suggestions met with a raised eyebrow at best. *Freya* and *Runa* came up the most often. She groaned in irritation when she heard *Sonnhild,* and *Hedwig* made her burst out laughing.

They didn't agree on *Johanna* until four hours after the birth, before which the baby was simply known as *it.* They came home from the clinic in silence, Ludger carrying the plastic bag containing the placenta, Paula holding Johanna.

She didn't know why the courage for another home birth had deserted her. She'd managed the first without any problems.

Had it been Judith's tales about stalled labor, umbilical cords that got wrapped around necks, a lack of oxygen, disabilities and death? Or was it a case of defying Ludger?

Once home he went straight to the fridge and put the placenta in the freezer compartment. Then he fetched Leni from the neighbors. She raced to Johanna, who was asleep in the baby seat. Delighted, she touched her tiny sister's hands, head and nose, and eventually Ludger had to carry her away to avoid upsetting Johanna's sleep.

Paula went to bed immediately, exhausted by the sight of Ludger. In the hospital car park he'd strapped the baby seat in the back and then gotten into the passenger seat. He didn't see any reason to drive instead of Paula. It was her car and he wanted as little to do with it as possible.

In fact Ludger drove the black Volvo precisely twice during the course of their marriage. The first time was on the way to the hospital when Johanna was born, the second on the way to her funeral.

That was in June. The sun shone fiercely and the entire city was full of German flags: football fans celebrating the World Cup victory. As the air-conditioning in the Volvo wasn't working, Ludger opened all the windows. The warm summer breeze caressed their heads and wafted in the sweet fragrance of the lime trees. The car was covered in honeydew. The handles were sticky, the windows filthy, but Ludger ignored them. He drove without switching on the windshield washer.

Bees and butterflies circled them at the cemetery, and hundreds of rhododendrons lined the paths and graves. Their flowers had withered some time ago and their leaves hung limply due to the sustained period of drought. It was the longest day of the year. The summer solstice. The eve of their fifth wedding anniversary.

Paula took in every breath of wind, every rustling leaf, every insect, but stared straight through the other people there. Ludger was holding Leni's hand. There was no life in his face.

*

Two days before she died Johanna had been vaccinated.

We're going to the doctor's today, Paula said, without interrupting what she was doing. *Hanni's getting an injection.* Johanna was sitting on Ludger's lap, slapping her plate with her hands. She liked the clattering sound, and she laughed and whooped, her round little body becoming ever more animated. Ludger's left arm was wrapped around her tummy, and with his right hand he tried to lift the coffee cup to his lips without spilling any. He'd been listening and narrowed his eyes. Paula knew that expression and took no notice of it. As she chopped up fruit and vegetables for Leni and made her some rolls for school, Ludger explained in his calm voice that good hygiene and living conditions rather than vaccinations were responsible for the control and even eradication of many illnesses. And when she took Johanna from him to get her dressed, he said that he'd heard of children being brain damaged or handicapped after vaccinations. *Do you want to go to the appointment instead?* she asked tetchily. *Are you going to be the one who stays at home when the children are sick? Are you going to look after them when they've got whooping cough or measles?*

Hastily, and without waiting for a response, Paula wrapped Johanna in the baby sling and left the apartment. Her colorful, ankle-length summer dress billowed in the breeze as she walked. She took her sunhat off and held it protectively over Johanna. They arrived at the practice on time.

Later he claimed he'd objected.

Later still he was sure he hadn't even been told about it.

*

Paula was wearing her summer dress with the large floral pattern on the day Johanna died, too. The apartment was suddenly full of people. The duty forensic pathologist examined the balcony, the place of death, to rule out the possibility of a crime. A psychologist sat beside Paula. The doctor on call, who had pronounced the child dead, sat opposite. He asked questions about what had happened that day and on previous days, and Paula replied in a monotone. She wanted to do everything the right way. Perhaps the child would open her eyes when all the questions had been answered. If she stayed strong, the nightmare might come to an end.

Johanna screamed for hours after the vaccination. She was burning hot, refused to drink or eat, and nothing could pacify her. She only slept when Paula gave her a syrup to bring down her temperature and relieve the pain. When she woke, she started screaming again. The next day her temperature had gone, but the child lay lethargically in her bed; it looked as though she was sleeping with her eyes open. She was staring at the ceiling, devoid of any expression, making no sound. She wouldn't play or laugh and didn't try to catch Paula's eye. Johanna hung limply on her arm and when Paula laid her down, she stayed in exactly the same position. The pediatric doctor assured her that it was just exhaustion after the fever.

On day three Johanna died.

Paula had put her on the balcony and she'd fallen asleep in a nest of blankets and cushions. When the child hadn't moved two hours later, Paula, who'd been reading on a lounger beside her, bent down and stroked her cheek. Johanna's skin felt cool, even though it was a pleasant seventy-seven degrees outside.

Paula knew at once.

She grabbed the baby and lifted her up. Pressed her against her body and screamed. Laid her back down and started giving mouth-to-mouth resuscitation. Ran to the telephone to call the emergency doctor. Called Ludger as she kneeled beside Johanna, shaking so badly that in the end she dropped the phone.

*

There was no strategy to combat the grief.

It was uncontrollable, unpredictable, limitless. For every other emotion in her life Paula had found a coping mechanism. Not for this one. The torpor of the first few weeks was the easiest part. The period when the realization was only in her head and hadn't yet spread to her heart. It didn't hurt yet; it was still abstract. Although the tiny creature had been buried, the bed was empty and the toy clock silent, the pain was lying in wait. But she suspected that it was collecting itself, growing bigger and preparing to strike.

✳

Ludger lived alongside her almost silently. He was there and also not there. He spent most of the time reading. The printer was permanently spitting out paper. Books and texts piled up around the desk and Ludger sat among them. He barely slept and ate little. Not for one moment had he believed the pathologist's conclusions: sudden infant death syndrome. Apparently, no abnormalities had been found in Johanna's brain to suggest any link with the vaccination. Apparently it was pure coincidence. It had no underlying cause and no one was to blame. And thus there was no sense to it.

But that couldn't be right. An eight-month-old infant doesn't die for no reason, with no blame, no sense. The agonizing uncertainty gave way to pure conviction. The search for the truth was over. The guilt was established.

He rarely worked now and barely earned any money. His eye for all those things that were unnecessary, useless, and immoral had become keener, as had his willingness to be consistent. He no longer took on jobs that conflicted with his ideals. He was scornful of his colleagues and wasn't interested in their arguments. He didn't want to hear about their wives and children and material needs that needed taking care of.

The architectural practice Brinkmann & Krohn fell apart. The sign was changed and the name Krohn removed from the headed paper.

To begin with Paula tried to get close to him. She would lay her head in his lap and find peace there. But Ludger did not return any of her caresses. He let it happen stiffly, and after that she kept her distance.

She responded silently and helplessly to Leni's cheerfulness. She didn't return her child's smiles, nor any of the joy in her eyes.

When the pain arrived, it was wild. Sometimes her crying sounded barely human. She was shocked by the sounds coming from within her, and there was fear on the face of her husband and daughter.

Every morning when she awoke she felt the horror. Every morning she wished it were evening—the day over, sleeping pills taken, the heavy curtain drawn. She didn't want to die, but she was unable to live. She wanted to forget, but that wasn't possible. And when Ludger uttered the words that ended their marriage, she was surprised that the darkness that surrounded her was no blacker than it had been before.

Johanna's death was your fault, he said one day. He stood in the kitchen doorway, spoke these words, turned around, and left.

✳ ✳ ✳

They lay silently side by side for a while.

I'm a lucky man, Wenzel says. *I've only just met you.*

She reaches for his hand and puts it on her tummy.

Later they dress and go into the kitchen.

He scrubs the vegetables, she gets the knife for him, washes the meat, pats it dry, and he cuts it into strips. He sets the table while she fries the meat and steams the vegetables. They don't get in each other's way. When he passes her, his hand strokes her arm.

They eat.

They drink wine and water.

They put the cutlery and crockery in the dishwasher.

They drink coffee.

They lie on the sofa and read.

They put their books down.

Three hours till Leni gets back . . .

They quickly remove their clothes, his hands glide over her hair, her neck, and down her back. He always wants to have a good look at everything. He always takes his time.

Paula's body reacts immediately to the touch of his hands, his lips, his tongue. She is not afraid of articulating her desires.

✳ ✳ ✳

Seventeen months after Johanna's death and just a few weeks after their divorce, Ludger went to Copenhagen to stay with friends. This time away was supposed to bring some resolution, a reorientation. The six weeks he'd planned became two years.

He missed Leni's sixth and seventh birthdays, the time she fell out of a tree and broke her right arm, her starting school, the first thing she wrote in cursive writing—*I lov you Mama*—a mass of lost teeth and new ones, and her first gallop on Judith's horse.

He would ring about once a week to speak to Leni. The phone calls only lasted a few minutes. Apart from *Yes, No,* and *Good,* Leni seemed to have nothing to say to her father. Paula didn't do anything to remedy this. Let him feel how quickly he could become estranged and how unimportant he was.

Her parents lent a hand to begin with. They brought Leni back to Naumburg for the weekend, went on visits to the zoo, and took short trips to the Ore Mountains or Saxon Switzerland. Paula's mother did what had to be done and she did it in the same way she had raised Paula and her brothers. Dutifully, uncomplainingly, and without any apparent emotional involvement. Her father treated her with friendly helplessness.

The rift occurred at Easter, almost two years after Johanna's death.

During the journey to Naumburg the wind whipped sleet against the windows of the train, and in the car from the station to her parents' house Paula saw the cathedral covered in a thick flurry of snow. Just before they got there her father told her not to be shocked, but they had other guests.

On the carpet in the sitting room sat two girls with long, black ponytails. They were speaking in Arabic and playing with Paula's old dolls. The television was on, and a man and woman with a headscarf sat bolt upright on the sofa, staring at the screen. A teenager was sitting at the table. In front of him was a reading primer that he stared at with concentration.

In his armchair her father retreated behind a book.

Paula's mother had been socially engaged before. She'd spent every free moment of her time helping the pastor, she'd sung in the church choir and given comfort to the residents of the local care home. While Paula and her brothers were fighting at home she never missed an opportunity to care for others.

Paula had nothing against these foreigners from Iraq and Afghanistan. The food was good too. Instead of the traditional roast there was hummus and baked eggplant, yogurt with garlic, couscous and lamb meatballs.

They all sat together at the table. The room was overheated, the wood-burner was blazing away and the snow was falling outside.

Paula! her mother said out of the blue. *Your problems aren't unique. These people*, she said, opening her arms wide, *have been through the most terrible times. You should get involved too. You'll see how quickly you feel much better.*

Paula studied the Iraqi woman and the girls, she looked the Afghani boy in the eye and he immediately lowered his gaze, and she stared at the man, who pretended not to notice.

Then she got up, took Leni by the hand, and left.

Her father was about to follow her, but one glance from her mother stopped him in his tracks.

✻

Paula coped.

She got up, brushed her teeth, made breakfast, put on lipstick,

went to work, and sold books. In the afternoons she helped
Leni with her homework, took her round to friends and to her
recorder lessons, read to her in the evenings, and then went
to bed soon after herself. She got up again, brushed her teeth,
made breakfast, put on lipstick, went to work, and sold books.
She learned to control her tears and never wept in front of her
child. She regularly invited people round to bring some life into
the household. She kept the apartment tidy, the clothes ironed,
and the plants on her balcony grew and prospered.

In the evenings she would sit at the dining table as if she'd
been switched off, her gaze fixed on the grain of the wood

She saw only a few of her old friends. When people around
her got married, had children, built houses, she couldn't share
in their pleasure. The only person Paula tolerated was Judith.
But even Judith couldn't understand what it meant to have lost
a child. A child that had never been born was less painful than
one who was dead.

Paula fell away from normal life. Her baby's death distanced
her from the average person. Her pain remained unshared. It
was like a cake that grew, and she ate and ate without it ever
getting smaller. Everything had to be measured against her suffering. Hardly anything passed the test. What were a few sleepless nights because a baby was teething? At least it was alive.
Any complaints were forbidden.

Nobody could compete with death. It was always greater.

Paula began to miss Ludger.

He'd been away long enough now for her to see him in a different light. His faults faded into the background while his good

points came to the fore. His boyish smile. His way of looking up at her diagonally, the feeling of security in his arms. Nobody was protecting her. Nobody asking how her day had been. Nobody doing the shopping. Nobody sleeping beside her. There was nobody she could relate to.

She looked at others with envy. Feeling the pressure of external circumstances, she approached Ludger again. The reliability of a bad marriage was still reliability.

Paula was both excited and frightened by Ludger's calls to Leni. When the telephone rang on Friday evenings, her heart would pound with such force that she found it difficult to breathe. One wrong word from him would put an end to her desire. But this desire was the most dynamic feeling she'd had in ages. All day long she would rehearse the words she wanted to say to him. At work she fine-tuned her phrases, and occasionally her colleagues let her know when they saw customers whispering as she muttered to herself among the bookshelves.

In her mind, what she said to Ludger would make him come back. He would apologize and heal everything that still hurt. He would take back his accusation that she was to blame for their child's death and it would be as if he'd never said it. But as soon as she heard his voice, she choked.

Hi, it's Ludger. Could you get Leni for me, please? These were his words every time. She would put the receiver down and call her daughter.

The conversation that put an end to her desire took place one Sunday afternoon. Paula liked to stay at home on Sundays. All that obliged her to leave the apartment were the trips to the playground. She would sit apart from the other parents, wearing large sunglasses even on gloomy days, and observe what was going on. Little knots would cluster around individual children, most were accompanied by both parents, a few by just their mother or father. The full strength of family relationships hung in the air, and sometimes Paula fantasized about shooting all these people dead, one by one.

That day she sat for two whole hours alone on a bench at the edge of the playground. While Leni practiced swinging off the climbing frame, Paula read Tolstoy's *Resurrection*. Back in the apartment, she let Leni watch four episodes of "Heidi," shut herself in the bathroom and lay down flat on the floor. Nothing was more exhausting than maintaining a façade with no support to underpin it.

Later she cooked spaghetti carbonara and drank a glass of red wine. The telephone rang during dinner.

I need to talk to you, Ludger said.

Her name was Filippa. He'd met her more than a year earlier.

*

The sickness seemed to follow logically.

When she awoke in the hospital, saw the catheter on the back of her hand and the drip stand beside her bed, she still thought her condition was linked to pneumonia.

She remembered her doctor listening to her chest, suspecting she might have pneumonia and telling her to get an x-ray at the radiology clinic as soon as possible. She'd tried to memorize everything he was saying and was surprised at how long it took to button up her blouse, put on her cardigan, and wrap her scarf around her neck. She went to reception, where the nurse handed her the referral note. She took it and stood rooted to the spot as she came out in a cold sweat all over. Then everything went black.

She was alone in the room. The door was slightly ajar and she could hear footsteps as well as a patient's wheelchair being wheeled down the corridor. She tried to push the duvet away, but couldn't. She was too weak. Too weak to move a duvet, too weak to raise her hand, too weak to speak. For some minutes she trembled and wept. Then the door opened and a doctor came into the room complete with entourage.

When her visitors had moved on, she tried to get her thoughts in order.

Leni was with Judith. She was fine.

Everything else finally made sense: the weird changes over the past few months, Judith's concerned looks and her urgent insistence on a variety of tests.

Paula had refused and had kept her distance from Judith.

In the end her colleagues remarked how brown she'd become. She'd noticed herself, of course. She saw it first on her hands. Only the skin on the tops of her fingers had remained pale. On her face the discoloration was patchy, extending from her nose across her cheeks and forehead.

Despite this she didn't do anything about it. Whatever it was, she didn't care. When she felt more and more jaded, she put this down to grief. And when she could no longer work, she thought she was depressed. And when she succumbed to one infection after the other, she thought her body was rejecting life.

In some respects she was right.

The Addisonian crisis almost killed her. Rapidly sinking hormone levels had caused the collapse at the doctor's office. She lay in a coma for two days. Her adrenal cortex had practically stopped producing cortisol. Any infection became potentially lethal. Never had she been so close to death.

*

When Ludger came back, Julianna's death was several times older than her life had been. Forty-one months of death versus eight months of life. If they were tossed onto a pair of scales, death would catapult the scrap of life high into the air.

When he arrived with Filippa on an unusually cold December day to pick up Leni, Paula looked with indifference at the friendly, round face of this woman she'd never met, at the messy blond hair, the short mauve dress, the chunky walking shoes and woolen tights, the huge, hand-knitted scarf, then back to the curiously elated face with its rosy cheeks.

A second glance almost took Paula's breath away. Filippa's belly was clearly bulging beneath the dress. She pushed Leni into the hallway, turned away without saying good-bye, and slammed the door shut.

She lay on her bed for a while, gazing out of the window. The outside thermometer read minus eleven. All the same this day would stay in her memory, different from any of the other days of the year. They had all blended into one, punctuated only by a few hours of restive sleep. Paula had carried out her duties in silence until finally she was able to sleep again. When Leni was with friends, Paula would fall into a vegetative state and only woke again when Leni was about to come back. She had spent whole days almost motionless on the sofa, watching American series, allowing herself to be lulled into a doze by the murmur of a foreign language. She kept losing her sense of time and the needs of her body, eating and drinking just enough to stay alive.

That day, too, the temptation to simply lie there was huge. Idle dozing would put her in that realm between sleeping and waking, drowsing as if under the influence of a mild anesthetic.

She closed her eyes and waited for the redemptive feeling of subsiding pain. The wind gusted around the roof, tugging at the gable and whipping the remains of dried leaves past the window and up into a colorless sky.

But Paula's heart was racing.

She got up again hurriedly, put on her lambskin shoes, coat, and a headscarf, and went down the stairs.

The wind was icy, the pavement glassy. Taking care not to fall, she walked to the grocer's. She bought milk, butter, paprika, and eggs, gathering up the money and putting the things in her cloth bag with irritating slowness under the watchful gaze of the shop assistant. She heard the man behind her huff and shuffle his feet. He wanted to pay for his things, he wanted her gone, but she couldn't do it any faster, her hands refused to obey. As if the connection to her brain were damaged, as if only fragments of information were being passed on. *Get moving, feet,* she thought, and was astonished when they did just that.

That icy winter wind again. She screwed up her eyes. Forward, step by step, slowly but surely. Before her, the road heavy with traffic. The cars passed her quickly in endless convoys with barely any gap. She stood right on the edge of the curb, her toes poking slightly over it. Lights, noise, wind. Paula raised her head, turned it a little to the left, and saw the lorry. It was driving at speed, it wouldn't stop. *Just one more step,* she thought.

The lights, the wind, and then a child of Leni's age. Right beside her. The girl leaned forward, glanced back and forth, then looked as if she were about to dash across the road. Paula reached out with both hands. She pulled the girl back roughly and grabbed her by the shoulders. *You can't just run across the road. You could have been killed!* she hissed. But the girl wriggled from her grasp. *I wasn't going to,* she said. *I was only looking.*

The lorry had passed. Paula's legs were trembling.

Slowly she walked back to the pedestrian lights, step by step along the frozen pavement, taking care not to fall.

Back home, she switched on the radio.

She listened to the news in the hope of hearing of something that was worse than her own life. Whenever she thought she'd never be able to enjoy a moment of happiness again, the distant victims of wars, natural catastrophes, starvation, poverty, and illness helped. On that day, however, the world seemed to be taking a break.

At six o'clock on the dot Ludger rang the bell, bringing Leni back. She was beaming. *May I come in?* he asked. Paula nodded feebly.

There ought to have been a lot to discuss as they sat opposite each other, forty-one months after Johanna's death. But Paula's gaze remained fixed on the table.

It had been built by Ludger.

It was a large, sturdy, beautiful table. *A table for eternity*, he'd said at the time. *This is where our children will eat and play.*

Those were the thoughts going around in her head as she sat there, staring at the grain and sensing Ludger's eyes on her. She remembered how she'd wanted this man to use her body. She hadn't wanted to decide anything, to have to say anything; she'd just wanted to follow instructions and be aware of her feelings.

Leni had been at school and Paula had opened the door to the man, the first of many. They greeted each other with a simple *Hello*, then she went over to the table. She was wearing a white nightie and nothing beneath it. She didn't want to speak. She didn't make coffee, didn't offer him wine, all she gave was herself.

He pushed her against the table and ran his hands from her waist down over her hips. There was an appreciation in this that Paula had long missed.

If Ludger had known . . .

But he knew nothing.

There should have been so much to discuss now they were finally sitting face-to-face. But Paula only raised her eyes, looked at Ludger, and told him he could see Leni on a regular basis if he liked. If he left his address and telephone number, she'd get in touch.

Is that all you've got to say to me? he asked. Paula nodded. Then she lowered her gaze and listened to his silence.

✳ ✳ ✳

Wenzel always brings her back

Their first conversation took place in the forest. They were standing on the platform of a viewing tower, beneath them the city and the broad green belt that extended in all directions. For weeks they'd been passing each other on their morning runs. Always at the same place. At some point he raised his hand in greeting when their paths crossed, later he murmured a *Good morning!* and smiled, then one day he appeared beside her rather than coming from the opposite direction and asked whether he might run with her for a while.

Paula's focus had become more precise; it had, as it were, shifted from somewhere in the distance to close-up. She saw the world around her differently now, noticed details she'd overlooked before, ever in expectation of bigger, greater things. As she ran she could feel the consistency of the ground, the exertion of individual muscles, the rhythm of her breathing, and she stopped shutting off the outside world with headphones. In one such moment of heightened perception, Wenzel came running into her life, literally.

And they ran together. Their feet touched the ground at the same time, in the same rhythm. They talked about running, the good fortune of living in this city, and Wenzel told her that he knew almost every birdsong. When he heard a nightingale, he took her arm and they stopped. The male sang trills and runs without repeating himself, and Paula didn't think it strange to be listening to a bird singing in the forest with a man she did not know.

Later, up in the viewing tower, she agreed to run with him on the following days too.

One week later he invited her over for tea.

His apartment was exactly as she'd imagined it: wooden floors, books, paintings, a simple, functional kitchen with good appliances. The studio was the biggest room, and of all the photographs hanging there, one caught her eye immediately: a woman of around fifty, long dark hair, narrow, serious face, large eyes.

Maja, Wenzel said, *my wife*.

✳ ✳ ✳

Barely a hundred yards separated the graves.

First they visited his wife's grave.

Then they walked on, past the rhododendrons, the gravel crunching beneath their feet.

The peonies were blooming, the plot had been weeded, the earth hoed.

Paula didn't cry. She just wiped some dust from the gravestone, stood up, and felt for Wenzel's hand.

Then they left.

PART TWO

Judith

E very woman needs a Christian Grey type in her life . . .
Seriously?

As she skims his profile, Judith puts the riding crop on the table and unzips her chaps.

Manager, 39, lives in Radebeul, no interests apart from sports, nonsmoker, divorced, no pets, no children. He has a raffish look and the vanity is all too plain to see.

She flips her laptop shut, takes off her shoes and jodhpurs, dumps everything in the hall, and heads into the bathroom.

Judith rode for three hours today. On the meadow by the river near Grubnitz, she really let the mare run. She bridged the reins, assumed the galloping position, and off they flew. There's no better way to describe it. When the horse stretches long and flat at full gallop, when the wind burns her eyes, when she feels the animal exhausting its energy.

In the shower she scrubs her back with a brush. Her hair lies wet and heavy on her shoulders. The oil she rubs in smells of birchwood. Judith loves this time, after exercise—feeling her warm muscles as she massages oil into damp skin.

She dries herself, puts on a T-shirt, then logs in again.

Doctor, 45, with own horse. Gelding, paint horse. Very beautiful, not too big.

Judith sends him a smile but no photograph.

Project manager, 46, describes himself as successful, striking, and masculine. His best quality: having empathy in spades. He has sent a smile but there's no photo.

Judith lights a cigarette. She gets up and opens the window, then writes:

Dear successful, striking, masculine man, empathy is the ability to read another person's feelings. Anybody claiming to have empathy "in spades" strikes me as suspicious.

She adds a winking smiley and clicks send.

Judith smokes serenely, not hastily like those nicotine addicts. In her search preferences she chose nonsmoker and no desire to have children. She's generous about age. They can be between thirty-five and fifty-five, although a fifty-five-year-old must have quite a bit to offer to make up for the age difference. She's a doctor, she's familiar with the problems men can have over the age of fifty. By then a hard, sustained erection is an improbable bonanza. Like a lottery win. But she doesn't do the lottery.

Project manager, 46, has answered.

I already feel sorry for your future partner, he writes.

A touchy subject, clearly, she answers promptly.

Go and see a psychologist! he comes back.

She dismisses him with the stop button, then sorts the other recommendations by compatibility points. Anyone with less than a hundred is of no interest.

Doctor, 45, scores 107. She smooths back her wet hair, pours water and apple juice into a glass, and clicks on the result.

Your match with KKTR005F is promising. Your personalities fit together well and in a relationship with KKTR005F you can expect your tastes and habits to have much in common. You will certainly feel comfortable together. Besides, you share many interests and hobbies—a real plus. You will not have any difficulty organizing your leisure time. We recommend you contact KKTR005F.

His horse *is* rather beautiful.

Good proportions, tobiano coloring, a bold expression.

In terms of gender roles in the context of a relationship, his feminine side outweighs his masculine one by 104 points to 85.

The scale runs from 60 to 140.

At 117 points, Judith's masculine side is more pronounced than that of the average man. *Could work,* she thinks. She knows her fellow doctors. Most of them don't like to be dominated, but this one appears to be an exception.

He sends back a smile and a photo. Bald head, bright eyes, open laugh, muscular. *Why not?* she thinks and goes to blow-dry her hair.

Hey, you, she writes to him later. Where do you work? Hospital or clinic? I like your horse. Shall we go for a ride? Regards, J.

The most difficult thing about meeting up with men you don't know is the effort of having to explain yourself, always having to start from scratch, there being no existing reference points. It's a real feat, on top of which there's the queasiness for the hour beforehand and the stale taste of futility afterward.

The second-most-difficult thing is the lack of ambiguity.

There's no doubt about the intent. Each person allows the other to gaze deeply into their own neediness.

Doctor, 45, writes back.

Hey, J, how about a coffee on Sunday afternoon? I'm an anesthetist working in the university hospital. My horse can't be ridden at the moment. I'll tell you more when we meet. Shall we say 3 p.m. in Südvorstadt? Café Grundmann? Regards, Sven.

You can't blame anyone for their name, Judith thinks as she replies.

I'm on call in Nordwest, but they say it's going to be a nice day, which usually means there's less to do. 3 p.m. could work. Shall we swap numbers?

Immediate answer.

No, too soon for me. I've had bad experiences.

I know, I understand! she writes back, thinking of her first time.

Lawyer, 40, divorced, 1 child—(not living with him)—nonsmoker, cat.

He'd suggested they meet at the Monument to the Battle of the Nations and from there take a stroll across the cemetery.

Within a few minutes he'd already steered the conversation to serious topics. He wanted his partner to share his political orientation, which meant: conservative.

Judith didn't see any point either in wasting time and energy on someone with different political opinions. When she asked what was at the heart of his conservative thinking, lawyer, 40, raised his eyes to heaven, then looked at a grave to his left, as if the answer lay down below with the dead.

Pessimism, he said. *More precisely, a pessimistic view of people.*

Voilà, she said, *that's something to work with.*

They passed the plot where Johanna was buried and discussed concepts like courage and honor, which curiously he kept coming out with. The rhododendrons were in peak bloom. They intruded boisterously into Judith's consciousness, and although she was listening to him, her mind was far away. Noticing this, he began to speak louder. His voice competed with the wind, the birds, and Judith's memory of the little body in the little coffin. Johanna had been eight months old.

The louder he spoke, the reedier his voice became, and although everything he said sounded logical and ordered, and while his sharp mind definitely appealed to her, she suddenly wished he would shut up. Judith looked at him. His gait was wooden, lumbering. Those legs would never dance. Those hips would remain inflexible. The intellect wasn't enough.

Lawyer, 40, was a mistake.

Judith recalled with disgust the tongues of intelligent men that had been thrust too far into her mouth. Men who ran companies or held political power but knew astonishingly little about the female anatomy.

She rapidly said her good-bye at the cemetery, but the relief was short-lived. For two whole months he wrote her emails, sent flowers or text messages with all manner of cultural suggestions. The only thing that stopped this enamored man was a letter from her lawyer headed *Stalking.*

As she's waxing her legs another message arrives from Sven as well as a thumbs-up from a professor, 48. **Love your profile**, it says. There is no photograph.

Judith wearily clicks on his profile. The blurred outlines of his photo suggest he's somewhat overweight. Hobbies: computers and golf.

Since when is being a professor a career? she writes, and the reply comes less than a minute later. **I don't need your disrespectful comments. Best of luck. You're going to need it!**

Her legs stiff with wax, she's sitting on a towel on the living-room floor. **Men like you don't have a future!** she writes.

She sends a stop button and reads what Sven has written.

Shall we stick with 3 p.m. tomorrow? I'll be punctual. Sven.

The pain when she pulls the wax away from her legs is not unpleasant. Beethoven's piano sonata no. 29 is playing in the background. With skin now as smooth as a baby's, she lies down on the sofa, her head beneath the window. The sun shines directly onto her face.

Every time a man took off his shoes and lay on this sofa, it was over. It was the moment that signaled the end of all the effort, the moment when she was captured.

She knows she's a beautiful woman. Her skin is still smooth, her hair thick and shiny, her teeth straight and white. Botox helps combat the small lines between her eyebrows.

Unlike Paula, in whose face you can read everything.

She's rung twice already and her number appears on the display again. Judith stares at the telephone until it stops ringing. She interprets the slight cramp in her tummy as a sign that she still has a conscience. But she can't talk to her today. Today she can't cope with any gloom.

Paula is like an abyss, a deep, black hole into which you cast reason, patience, and love. All of it sinks to the depths without producing even the slightest echo. Johanna's death changed everything.

Sometimes she looks after Paula's older daughter. They drive out into the country to see the horse. The girl is allowed to brush down the mare and lunge a few rounds. She's not gifted at riding. She hops around on the back of the horse and holds the saddle tight rather than feeling the rhythm and allowing herself to move with the animal. But Judith feels sorry for Leni. She's not yet a teenager and already she has a grown-up face.

The third movement of the piano sonata is almost at the best part. Judith gets up, takes the score from the shelf, and follows the piece. Just before the last section of the third movement the telephone rings again.

It's Hans, who used to be her boss when she was training to be a specialist. In his depressive phases he never gets in touch; when he's manic, they meet several times a week.

He's a god in bed. She knows how that might sound, but it doesn't alter the fact that he *is* a god in bed.

Three children, a short, thin wife, but that's irrelevant. After all, Judith has no intention of living with him. She doesn't want him to take his shoes off and lie on the sofa. She doesn't want him to ease up, stop making an effort, hole up with her.

Hans, she says, *do you have the hots for me?*

He laughs. *If only you knew . . .*

Tell me, she whispers.

She leans back and listens. When he stops speaking and breathes more quickly, she says: *Come over this evening.*

But Hans doesn't come. The short wife, who's carrying child number four, needs him. And whenever she needs him he's there.

*

The light in the bar is muted.

Her eyes scan the room. Just couples and groups. Tom recommends a Weissburgunder from Baden. She nods and he pours her a glass.

How was your week? he asks.

Tiring, she says. *I had a hundred and seven patients on Thursday. Can you imagine?* She takes a sip of her wine and shakes her head.

And how's the nag?

She laughs. *The nag's got spring fever even though it's summer. She almost threw me off today, but I love her all the same.*

And the men? He grins.

She waves a hand dismissively. *The men . . .*

Tom polishes glasses while they chat. His eyes are blue, his lashes thick and black. Young women flirt with him and Judith wonders whether she's old enough to be his mother. His beard is neatly trimmed, his hair shaven at the sides, while at the back he wears it in a ponytail. His body looks strong and healthy, with well-defined muscles. But the appearance is deceptive.

She is certain that in a real emergency Tom would be a failure. He has a vain and innocent look, and he is a pacifist, neutral. In her eyes he is no man at all.

Judith takes a cigarette from a silver case and goes outside with her wineglass. The other smokers stand in groups. Including one of her patients. A severe allergy sufferer, with chronic bronchitis and mild rosacea.

She turns away and leans against the wall. The traffic rushes past and the lime trees emit their sweet fragrance, which can be overpowering when mixed with the cocktail of other urban smells. Swifts fly overhead, always in groups, incredibly fast and shrieking shrilly. Soon they will leave the city and fly south of the equator without stopping. They will sleep on the wing and not all of them will make it.

Later she thinks about leaving the car there.

Even later she gets into the black Audi and races through the empty, night-time streets, Verdi arias blasting from the speakers.

As she unlocks the door to her building she hears footsteps behind her. Somebody pushes her into the hallway. It's Hans.

They rush up the stairs. In the hallway of her apartment he presses her against the wall, pushes up her skirt, pulls down her panties, and puts a hand between her legs. She stands still as he moves his fingers. He kisses her neck and keeps stroking her. He knows what to do, he knows every detail of her body.

She sits down on the edge of the bed and leans back. *I've missed you*, she says.

When he leaves, she falls asleep straightaway. But she's awake again two hours later. It is four o'clock in the morning.

She gets up at five, puts on her running gear, jogs down the stairs and along the street into the park.

At seven she's sitting at the breakfast table, freshly showered. Her shift is beginning.

At eight o'clock the driver is at the front door, a medical student called Sebastian.

You can call me Basti, he tells Judith. She decides to ignore his audacity, taking it as a compliment instead.

At a quarter past eight they climb the steps to a modern apartment.

Woman, eighty-two, urinary tract infection with a temperature.

At half past nine a dehydrated seventy-year-old. The entire apartment reeks of diarrhea. Overflowing ashtrays, closed windows. Judith fills out the emergency admission form and tells Basti to let in some fresh air.

Back in the car she nods off and wakes up again to a song by The Doors: "People Are Strange." The student has turned up the volume and is nodding his head in time to the music.

Just before midday, a case of fainting. Woman, twenty-six, apparently undernourished. The apartment looks as if nobody lives there. On the wall in the hallway, a print of Van Gogh's sunflowers; palm-tree wallpaper in the bedroom. Judith has the woman admitted to hospital, making a note that she strongly suspects anorexia.

The car radio is playing hits from the 1980s. She takes a CD from her bag and gives it to the student. *Would you mind?* she says. Pergolesi's "Stabat Mater" fills the car, changing the atmosphere at a stroke.

*

As a child Judith spent hours beside the organ in church. She liked nothing better than to be with her father while he practiced in the gallery. She found the liturgical organ music boring, but she loved the concert pieces. Wrapped in woolen scarves, she would sit on a lamb fleece and draw while her father played Bach and between pieces talked about the composer's life.

Her mother worked shifts at the hospital. Sometimes Judith didn't see her for days.

She was six when she began playing the piano herself. When she was twelve, she told a family friend how Astor Piazzolla's compositions had been influenced by his experience of listening to counterpoint in Bach's fugues.

Music was everywhere. She practiced the piano every day, often for several hours, and she sang in the children's choir with Paula.

Paula was her only friend.

They were very different. Paula was withdrawn and desperate to be accepted by the other girls; Judith was precocious, insolent, and totally uninterested in girls' things. The boys were intimidated by her sarcasm and the girls by her competitiveness. She often stood at the edge of the playground watching the other girls in groups, giggling, provoking the boys, their voices ratcheting up ever higher, their hair flowing in the breeze. Sometimes Paula stood beside her, watching too.

✳

They stop outside the house of the next patient. A villa by the park.

Man, fifty-six, heavy smoker.

A substantially younger woman anxiously explains that the man has chest pains. He didn't want an ambulance. Judith is requested to handle the matter discreetly.

Without a blood test Judith cannot rule out a heart attack, and his blood pressure is far too high. She gives him some fast-acting medicine and begins the process of having him admitted to a hospital. When he refuses, she doesn't enter into a discussion. She tells him of the risks, has him sign the refusal, and leaves.

Time for lunch, she says to Basti, who's fiddling around with his phone.

Then she cranks back the seat and closes her eyes.

Shortly before 2 p.m. Judith knows that Sven will wait in vain. She doesn't have a number for him and there's no time to cancel via e-mail.

Doctor, 45, will sit on his own in Café Grundmann today.

Basti drives speedily to the next patient.

A common cold. Irritated, Judith writes the woman a prescription and leaves the apartment with a terse good-bye.

Now she remembers the trouble she's in with the medical association. She needs to draft a response, urgently. In the last quarter she invoiced for too many consultations. They've run a plausibility check on her once before. The problem was ludicrous: getting too much done in too few days. But that's how her work is. Some days she arrives at the office at 7 a.m. and leaves around 8 p.m. Lunch is ordered in, followed by forty winks on the treatment table, and then she gets going again.

She has her mother to thank for this work ethos.

Just thinking of her mother makes her tired. These days she asks the C question every time they speak on the phone, the last being quite recently. *No, Mama,* she said, *there aren't any grandchildren on the way.* She heard the breathing on the other end of the line and knew exactly how her mother looked at that moment. Serious and gray, her hair—now thin—tied up in a bun, her eyebrows severely plucked, and always the same color lipstick. A brownish red that fell out of fashion long ago.

Then Judith drove to see her horse, brushing and grooming the coat until it shone and all the clumps of mud were gone, and combing the mane and tail until there were no more tangles. She treated ears and belly with insect repellent and finally took her out into the field, where the grain stood high and you could ride in the tracks of agricultural vehicles, the ears of corn whipping your legs. She urged the horse on, then let her gallop for a long time. The sweat ran down both of them and nothing else mattered.

In the car she flips down the sun visor and peers into the small mirror. The frown lines between her eyebrows are clearly visible again. She decides to make an appointment for an injection.

Basti stops outside a building that hasn't been refurbished. The smell in the stairwell reminds Judith of the apartment she shared with Paula for five years.

Paula and Judith—two late bloomers. At fourteen both were

still flat-chested, at fifteen they were the last girls in their year to start their periods, and at seventeen they had their first boyfriends.

Within the space of a few months, tall, pallid Paula developed into every boy's crush. Her appearance was striking: the green of her eyes, the red of her hair, her porcelain skin, and the soft, lithe way she moved. In comparison Judith was severe, sporty, androgynous.

When one of the boys took her hat off as he passed, expecting that she would run after him squealing, she just stood there, looking bored. This blatant sign of erotic interest was an insult to her intelligence. To Judith these boys seemed like small genetically programmed creatures. Poor, weak-willed beings who behaved without any self-control.

Her first boyfriend was her PE teacher.

Seventeen years older, married, one child.

She rings the bell. A man opens the door and invites her in. Piano music is coming from a room to the rear of the apartment. Judith recognizes the first movement of Beethoven's "Pathétique" sonata. The walls are covered with prints, drawings, and photographs.

A woman is lying in bed, a colorful cloth wrapped around her head. The bedside table is full of medicines. Feebly she raises her hand; she finds it hard to talk.

My wife, Maja, the man says, then introduces himself as Wenzel Goldfuss.

Judith sits down and listens to the man talk. Maja has late-stage breast cancer. She woke up in the night, feeling feverish.

She was unable to swallow and had a bad headache. She couldn't even make it to the bathroom on her own.

We don't want to go to the hospital, he says. *That's why we called the duty doctor.*

Judith takes her time with the examination. The woman must be around fifty. Chemotherapy has left her weak, and her weak immune system has allowed the severe infection to take hold.

She looks through the medicines on the bedside table and checks them for compatibility with the ones she is going to prescribe. *You need to consult the oncologist,* she says. *I should really have your wife admitted to the hospital right away.* Deep lines in the man's gaunt face run from his nostrils to his mouth. But his eyes are open and clear, and there is something vigorous and decisive about his body.

Tomorrow. I promise.

Judith nods. She regards most patients as minor wards who, in case of doubt, need to be dealt with strictly. These two, however, seem to know what they're doing. *If her condition worsens, especially if her temperature doesn't go down, then please call the emergency doctor,* she adds, handing the man the prescription.

The piano sonata has now reached the third movement and Judith guesses that Alfred Brendel is the pianist. Wenzel Goldfuss smiles for the first time.

You can hear that?

I almost became a pianist, she says with a shrug.

As she goes down the steps beside Basti she has an unsettling feeling. She's envious of the sick woman. Maja Goldfuss is going to die. But Judith has never sensed anything as strong as the bond between these two people.

They say nothing on the way to the next patient.

Basti is a good driver. No sharp braking, no excessive accelerating. He steers the car smoothly through the city. Judith closes her eyes and seconds later finds herself in a light sleep. During those long hospital weekends, on double shifts and night duty, she had to learn to make use of every break. Despite this she's never regretted having opted to study medicine.

Yes, she could have become a decent pianist, too. But the certainty that she'd never be anything out of the ordinary, that she'd never shine, made Judith not only abandon the qualifying examination, but give up the piano altogether.

When she first entered the auditorium in Leipzig—for a lecture on anatomy—she went all the way down to the front row, took a seat in the middle, unpacked her pen and notepad, and then looked her future lover in the eye.

✳ ✳ ✳

Friedemann Schwarz, married, two children.

They would meet in an apartment rented for the purpose. Normal first-semester life, the studying and the partying, passed Judith by. She shuttled almost exclusively between her room in the hall of residence, the German National Library, and the tiny attic apartment in the Waldstrassenviertel.

The bed was the heart of the apartment. Friedemann and she would look out through the angled window at the morning, afternoon, or night-time sky. Sometimes rain would pound the windowpane, sometimes the blazing sun would shine down on their sweaty bodies, and sometimes the glass was covered in snow. Then they would make love beneath the pale, shadowless, winter light and felt as if what they were doing had no connection to the world outside. Lying around the bed were all the things they needed for their lovemaking. In this apartment, this room, this bed, the usual rules did not apply.

When some observant girls spread the rumor that she was the professor's tart, she didn't deny it. Her effortless grasp of every subject alienated her from her fellow students anyway. She didn't join any study groups and never turned up to parties. The weekends were spent at a riding center on the outskirts of the city with a gelding called Herkules, whose owner was unable to come often enough to look after the horse.

Judith tended to prefer the company of the horse to that of other people.

After four semesters she got the top mark in her year in the preliminary medical examination. Friedemann was the first to hear about it. They celebrated with champagne in bed. Judith never asked him to leave his wife. All she wanted was the best of him, not the children, which weren't hers, nor the hatred of an abandoned and betrayed wife.

It was Friedemann who ended the affair. He never wanted to be tempted into this dark realm of his desire again. As a parting shot he told her that, in the past, a woman like her would have been burned as a witch.

Daniela Krien

* * *

Basti turns into a tree-lined street and double-parks.

A 1950s building, the smell of detergent in the stairwell, and spyholes in the doors; it feels claustrophobic.

Woman, seventy-one, high-necked white blouse, gray-blue pleated skirt.

On the bookshelves the works of Marx and Engels, the Russian classics, and the packaged canon of German literature. On the sideboard is the photograph of a man wearing an East German police uniform replete with badges. A black ribbon is taped around the upper-right corner. The apartment looks as if the woman has lived her whole life here. It would have been a privilege in GDR days. Good location, central heating, hot water.

Judith's home had been cold, she used to rip her tights on the damaged parquet floor, the old villa's windows weren't sealed, while the coal cellar was full of spiders and ghosts. Only in summer, when the conservatory doors were open and she could leap up from the piano and run into the garden, would she not have changed places with other people. When her parents' friends came for parties. When she was allowed to chat with them and have eggnog in a tiny cup made of chocolate. She loved talking to adults and not even her mother, who disliked her *precocious waffle* and would rather have stuck her with the other children, spoiled those summer evenings beneath old trees, where Judith would sit at a table with her father's musician friends.

As the woman describes her symptoms, it occurs to Judith

74

that it was people like her and the man in the picture who made life difficult for her parents. People with a party badge and the power that went with it. People who spread their toxic influence into every branch of the next generation—and into Judith's life.

When the woman describes her pains and shows the clusters of blisters on her lower back, Judith thinks of the damage that shingles can cause. Postshingles neuralgia can lead to severe, burning pain. Paralysis of peripheral nerves is not uncommon either.

She looks at the photo of the man again, then gazes into the old woman's tired eyes and imagines her mother checking the roster in the polyclinic and again finding her name down for night, holiday, and weekend shifts over the Christmas period. She recalls sitting once more beside Paula's family in the freezing cold church on Christmas Eve because her father was conducting the choir and her mother was on duty at the clinic.

Through the window she sees another modern block. It's no longer a privilege to live here.

Basti drops her home shortly after 7 p.m.

She makes tea, eats a banana, and opens her laptop.

A message from Sven.

Pity. We ought to have swapped numbers after all. Shall we try again tomorrow evening? Will you call me?

There is a smiley after his phone number.

Judith clicks on another message: Judge, 52, with photograph.

Dear stranger, it would be a pleasure to have the opportunity to invite you for a walk and a coffee afterward. I was most interested by

your profile. Our promising compatibility results leave me hopeful of a positive response. Yours, G.H.

Judith looks at his profile: six feet, nonsmoker, two children, none at home, exercises several times per week.

How does his perfect day begin? With the woman I love.

What is he allergic to? Broken promises and inconsiderateness.

Three things that are important to him: My children, my lover, and art.

She looks at his picture again. Fourteen years of visible age difference.

Despite this she checks her compatibility results with G.H.

Their gender-role balance is exactly the same, both of them scoring 104 points for My masculine side, and 109 for My feminine side. For How empathetic are you? the two of them both notch up an above-average 118.

Judith only gets 85 for Adaptability, whereas his score is 109.

In the categories Willingness to compromise, Introversion, Generosity, and Determination they deviate from each other by no more than three points.

She rarely has a result like this. G.H. gets a message.

Half an hour later she's in the car. At the petrol station she buys gummi bears, milk chocolate, a packet of cigarettes, and a few minutes later parks illegally outside Paula's house.

Paula opens the door. Her high cheekbones stick out prominently. She's wearing makeup and colorful clothes, but that means nothing. When she smiles, Judith glances at the child to see how Paula really is.

Leni is never far away from her mother. She usually sits

within sight of her, drawing or playing with her toy animals. Her favorites are elephants, tortoises, and hedgehogs. Today she seems relaxed, almost happy. She greets Judith, shows her delight at the sweets and then becomes absorbed in her game again, with a handful of gummi bears in her mouth.

It's a miracle that Paula is still alive. Judith has never seen a person fade away like this.

Sorry I didn't call you back yesterday.

Paula contorts her face into the fake smile that Judith cannot stand. She fills the kettle, takes two cups from the cupboard, puts a teabag in each, and says, *It's all so pointless.*

Judith lays her hands on Paula's shoulders. Then she tells her what she always tells her. That over time it will get better, that she has to force herself to focus on the positives, that one day she'll feel happiness again, fall in love. But Paula shakes her head. *I'll never have another relationship. I'm too damaged.*

Leni has interrupted her game. She sits quite still on the floor, listening. Then she gets up, goes over to Paula, and wraps her arms around her mother.

Judith turns away.

Later they smoke on the balcony.

Today, Judith says, *I witnessed true love.*

She tells Paula about Wenzel Goldfuss and his wife, Maja. She describes the tender caresses, the warm looks, and how natural it all was. *The wife is going to die,* she says, taking a deep breath and blowing the smoke into the evening sky. *But she didn't look unhappy.*

Paula smiles and takes a puff of her cigarette too. *We ought to have been smarter,* she says. *It's too late now. Now it's obvious that there's something wrong with us.*

Judith is offended by the *we.* But she doesn't delve deeper. She doesn't want to know what's wrong with her. Not today. They both stare at the evening sky.

When it's time for Judith to go, they hug.

Call me if anything happens! Judith says, turning around on the next landing, but Paula's door is already shut.

No answer from G.H.

Though he has been online.

She checks the compatibility results again. For the question How do you view the world? there are three categories: Instinct, Emotion, and Reason. His results stand out. Instinct and Reason score highly, way above average. By contrast, Judith's instinct is at a weak 81 points. For Emotion she is just about average. Only on Reason does she score more highly than him.

For Domesticity, both just scrape above 80, but for Desire for an ordered life they are at the upper end of average.

It's definitely possible to manipulate the psychological test underpinning these results, but out of genuine curiosity Judith was completely open and truthful in her answers. Although she was briefly horrified by the results, in the end she had to concede that the evaluation did correspond to her personality.

How often had she recklessly let men into her life, men she didn't even like? How often had reason deluded her into believing certain things that later turned out to be gross errors of judgment?

These days she mistrusts reason. It's capable of finding arguments for and against everything. Nothing has a value, nothing is absolute, everything is negotiable. Without regulation by instinct, reason and intellect are practically worthless.

Judith checks the time. It's almost 10 p.m. Still nothing from G.H.

The waiting is terrible. If they make her wait, she'll start getting interested in those men who have no appeal. She can't sleep, and reading is impossible too. Every thought is focused on that moment when the waiting will stop.

In the past, when she and Paula still lived together, even this was nice. They used to drink wine and entertain each other. And if it didn't work out with one guy, there was always another. Such dependability allowed them to cope with almost every setback. But then along came Ludger and he took Paula with him.

At around 11 p.m. Judith shuts her laptop and lies in bed, wide awake.

She needs to feel she's achieved something. She knows what an ongoing lack of dopamine and serotonin leads to: a weakened immune system. Unhappiness makes you ill, it's as simple as that.

Sometimes she's flabbergasted by the generosity of other women. How mild they are in their judgments, how gently they devote themselves to their husbands, how magnanimously they accept and overlook their weaknesses.

It's midnight when she gets to sleep, but just before half past three she is woken by her own crying. It's already morning when she falls again into a deep sleep.

✳ ✳ ✳

The waiting room is full by the time Judith arrives at the office a quarter of an hour late. She ignores Siegrun's reproachful looks. The younger of her two assistants wouldn't dare behave like that. Siegrun can because she is bringing up three children on her own and is indispensable to the office.

Good morning, everyone! We'll start right away! Judith calls out, before dashing into consultation room 1, putting on her doctor's coat, and washing her hands. The first patient's file is on the desk in front of her. She calls Frau Lichtblau over the intercom. Brida Lichtblau has problems sleeping and comes in with a stack of printed paper.

Have you finished the novel? Judith asks.

Brida says yes and drops the manuscript, held in a rubber band, onto the desk with a thump. *If you could read it by next week that would be wonderful. Please focus only on whether I've got the facts right.*

Judith nods. *So?* she says. *What happens now?*

If everything goes according to plan, it'll be out in a year.

Brida Lichtblau leaps to her feet. She strides to the door in her high-heeled suede boots, turns and says effusively, *Thanks a million!*

Her long plait is wrapped around her head like a crown. This old-fashioned hairdo looks like a disguise to hide the anger seething inside her. Brida slightly reminds Judith of herself. Of her own mimicry. Of episodes in her childhood when she lost control and let herself go wild. And of how her parents told her she was hard work, unpleasant, and made it difficult for others to like her. It wasn't any surprise, they said, that nobody wanted to be her friend.

But that wasn't true. Judith did have a friend. She had Paula.

There are no interesting patients for the rest of the morning.

Judith works through the appointments with her usual assurance. Only rarely does something get to her. She can't see how it's possible to show compassion hundreds of times a day. When the patients come in, she looks each of them in the eye, but she doesn't shake their hand until the end, when she can be sure it's highly unlikely they're carrying an infectious disease.

After a hurried lunch at the Vietnamese restaurant around the corner, she returns to the office. Siegrun is sitting at her desk in reception with a pile of magazines. In front of her are Tupperware containers with sandwiches and vegetable sticks. Judith smiles at her and goes into consultation room 1. She sits at her computer and checks to see whether G.H. has written back.

Nothing.

She looks at his profile again.

Under the heading One of my positive features, he has written: Others can be the judge of that, and for Two things I could never part with, he's put: Every object is replaceable, people aren't.

As she scrolls down, a message arrives from Sven.

You haven't sent a message or called. Have you lost interest? A rejection would have been polite. Sven.

She had actually forgotten Sven. Judge, 52, had effortlessly supplanted Doctor, 45.

I wish I could . . . not only pronounce judgment, but deliver justice, she goes on reading, then clicks back to Sven and writes: Dear Sven, I've just been so busy. How about this evening? 8 p.m. at Barcelona?

G.H. would like to meet the philosopher Robert Spaemann and as a first meeting place he suggests the large oak tree in the Rosental.

He doesn't provide a target of any sort, no opportunity for mockery. Without having met him Judith reckons she can take this man seriously.

Sven sends three laughing smileys and a Great, see you later!

G.H. is still silent.

The afternoon appointments begin with a typical case of honeymoon cystitis. This is followed by an elderly gentleman with breathing difficulties. His pulmonary function test is cataclysmic, so she sends him straight to the pulmonologist. Then come a female student with an irritable bowel, a mother of four with full-blown depression, an overweight old woman with reddened wrinkles, a man with two ingrown toenails, and a soprano with inflamed vocal cords.

By the end of the day there's still no message from G.H.

*

Sven is already there when Judith enters the bar. He gets up and comes over to meet her.

Hi, he says, *good to see you*.

Not tall, but sporty and attractive. A springy step and a firm but not exaggerated handshake. He helps her out of her coat and takes it over to the rack. Then Sven asks her whether she'd prefer to sit at a table or at the bar, if she'd like to have something to eat or just a drink, whether she's come straight from the practice, and is she not exhausted after work. He tells her he was only on duty till early afternoon today, after which he went for a ten-mile run and cleaned his apartment—I mean, he says with a wink, you never know who might pop by—then he arrived here early to get some good seats, and he's really glad to see her.

How's the horse? Judith asks when he pauses to draw breath. She browses the menu while Sven talks about the gelding's arthrosis, what supplements he feeds it, and what he's doing to combat the symptoms as quickly as he can—linseed oil, vitamins, zinc, and selenium—how he's doing regular groundwork exercises and hopes to be able to ride him again soon. Then he pauses and laughs; she finds the laugh quite appealing.

As Judith decides on Rioja and tapas, Sven talks about his weekly exercise routine. He works out every day and does not only the Leipzig triathlon, but the Hamburg, Berlin, and Munich ones, too.

He doesn't drink; she already knows that he's a nonsmoker.

Over dinner their chat is easy and relaxed. Judith orders another glass of wine, Sven another water. The conversation meanders with no particular aim, he skillfully avoids more profound topics, and there's something about him that Judith doesn't quite get. He has good skin, he's fit, he's got a healthy, positive mind. Why is he on his own? But turn the question on its head, and it also makes sense.

Ever since she's been on this dating site, she hasn't been able to shake off a niggling suspicion. There has to be something not quite right with men who rely on this method to find women. Just as there's something not quite right about her.

Sven takes his mobile from his bag, glances at it, and puts it away. Without further ado he asks if she'd like to come back with him. This offer doesn't usually happen at the first meeting. Judith sees a man two or three times before she sleeps with him. But the wine is having its effect and, feeling pleasantly relaxed, she nonchalantly agrees.

Sven came by bicycle. He tells her his address and says, *See you in a bit.*

As she's parking she sees him standing by the front door, his hands casually in his pockets. Despite the wine, Judith effortlessly maneuvers the car into a narrow space and follows him up to the fourth floor of an apartment block that looks as if it's been renovated very recently.

Sven takes off his shoes as soon as he enters his apartment and places them neatly in a black shoe rack. Judith takes off her pumps, too, and walks barefoot across the cold laminate to the sitting room. Her eyes take in a huge flat-screen television, a music system with large speakers, and shelves of CDs. There are hardly any books. When Sven comes back from the kitchen with a bottle of water and two glasses she wants to leave.

It's quiet. So quiet that when she crosses her legs and shifts her weight it makes a noise. The sofa is red and made of leather.

Can I show you something? Sven says, picking up a remote control.

An image appears on the flat-screen. Now Judith knows she *has* to leave.

The woman in the film has a whip in her right hand. Her voice is soft but firm.

I've got everything we need, Sven says.

Judith nods. She gently strokes his arm, then puts down her glass and leaves the apartment.

Before she starts her car she puts on the "Well-Tempered Clavier" and turns the volume up high. Preludes and fugues, absolute harmony, counterpoint, and polyphonic perfection are going to erase those images.

Judith pulls out of the parking space and puts her foot down. She is wide awake, speeding through the night as the "Prelude in C Major" makes that final, abjectly submissive expression on Sven's face fade. By the end of the "C Minor Fugue" she has arrived home. What she really fancies now would be to drive on and listen to all twenty-four paired movements that rise in pitch chromatically, and not stop until she's reached the end of the B minor.

She runs up the stairs, shuts the door behind her in relief, pours a vodka, and rolls a cigarette. Here in her apartment she's safe. There's no flat-screen television, no porn films, no cold laminate, and, most importantly, nobody else.

Judith logs on to the dating portal, blocks Sven's profile, ignores the new partner suggestions, and decides to take a break from the site. She's in bed before midnight, but she can't sleep.

*

On Tuesday evening she goes to the cinema with Hans, and then they shag half the night.

On Wednesday afternoon she meets Paula for a coffee, then takes Leni with her to see the horse.

On Thursday evening she rings her parents on the way to the equestrian center. She spends a good hour riding the horse, then drives home, has a shower, and later sits in her favorite bar reading Brida Lichtblau's manuscript. Judith doesn't recognize the barman. She asks after Tom and learns that he's gone traveling for a while, to Asia: Thailand and Myanmar. Brida has put Post-its on the relevant pages. The main character in the novel is a bipolar ER doctor; Judith does not recognize herself in this woman's life.

On Friday afternoon she loads the mare into the horse trailer and drives to the Dahlener Heide. For three hours she rides through forests, across meadows, and between fields, mostly walking and trotting. She meets two other riders, a couple with their dog, and a forester. She would have preferred nobody to have crossed her path.

She sleeps right through the night.

On Saturday morning she has a big breakfast of eggs and fruit, takes her time in the bathroom, and treats herself to a second cup of coffee and a cigarette. Then she wanders into the city center.

Judith meets Brida in a café. She talks through the corrections and listens to her problems. She's good at this—dissecting, analyzing, and ordering other people's relationships. She always knows what needs to be done, and Brida listens gratefully.

Later, Judith buys a pair of red lace-up ankle boots, a light-gray woolen coat, a claret scarf, and a batch of underwear. But even as the sales assistant swipes her credit card through the reader, Judith feels an emptiness. Back home, she carelessly puts the bags down by the coatrack.

Then she turns on the computer, puts on her headphones, and checks for messages as the opening bars of Beethoven's final piano sonata ring out.

Dear J., let me be honest with you. There was another woman on the site I was interested in, which was why I didn't reply. It struck me as really sleazy to communicate with two women in parallel, but I couldn't and didn't want to reject you outright because I'm genuinely interested in you too. The other woman is now history, so I'm writing to you again in the hope that I haven't mucked everything up. I'd very much like to meet you. Please get back in touch if you're not put off or even offended by my bluntness. I'm on vacation next week and can fit in with your plans. Best regards, G.H.

* * *

Judith wakes up.

Overnight an autumnal storm swept across the city, flinging branches against her window and wrenching the last leaves from the trees. She trudges into the bathroom, having to reach out to the wall for support. Her blood pressure is lower than usual. When the jet of water from the shower hits her breasts, she winces; her nipples are hard and sensitive.

Something soft has covered her face. She notices it as she

rubs lotion in; it's unsettling. She dabs serum around her eyes, but this morning the tiredness sticks to her. The light in the bathroom feels harsh. She turns it off and looks in the mirror again, turning her face from side to side, but the strange expression won't go away.

On the way to work she listens to Schubert's *Piano Trio No. 2*. The andante brings tears to her eyes. She pauses the CD, opens the window, and breathes in the cool morning air.

Something isn't right.

At the next set of lights she flips down the sun visor and looks in the mirror again. In her mind she runs through the list of yesterday's patients, their illnesses and the possibility that she might have been infected, but her symptoms are too vague for a diagnosis.

She parks the car and walks swiftly the last few feet to her practice, unable to rid herself of the curious sensation of feeling a more immediate connection to the world. She closes her eyes and opens them again, but nothing has changed. Her perception is still different from usual. As if the air were thicker and the information from her environment conveyed more clearly in this density.

The waiting room is already full, as ever. She sees forty-seven patients before lunchtime. Instead of her usual impatience toward those who don't want to go to work because they've got a cold, she writes generous sick notes. She has sushi delivered and works through her lunch break, examining some blood test results and fetching the files of those patients she will ask to return to the office. You don't pass on bad news over the telephone. She writes two short consultant's reports for courses of psychotherapy, both with the diagnosis F43.2—adjustment disorder following change or traumatic events with emotional impairment.

Judith has some alarming news to pass on to a woman of her age. The ultrasound was revealing, the tumor markers are high, the suspicions of cancer have been substantiated. Now she has to send the mother of two for an endoscopic ultrasound and a CT scan. If there is confirmation that she has pancreatic cancer, she won't have long to live. No doubt she'll be thinking more of her children than of herself. Judith has seen this so often. They're desperate to live for their children's sake. But there is little hope of this cancer being cured.

She reaches for a roll of sushi, dips it first in wasabi paste then in soy sauce, before putting it in her mouth.

There is this possible hypothesis: given a similar diagnosis, age, and general state of health, those patients with small children live on average longer than those that are childless.

What if it happened to her? The question throbs inside her head. Judith leaves the kitchen, crosses the waiting area, and opens the window. But the noises from the street don't drown out her thoughts.

She has forty-five minutes until the next patients arrive. Then everybody will want her to do her best again, miss nothing, not make a single mistake. She doesn't make any, and there's a more profound point to this. Something worth living for.

As soon as her workday is over she drives to the stables.

For half an hour she brushes down her mare and sees to the

hooves, then she saddles her, leads her into the arena, and sets up two low jumps. Ten minutes of warm-up riding, a few laps of gentle trotting, then she sits the trot and starts to gallop, riding a controlled working canter, first with her left hand, then her right, followed by a few volts and then she slows her to walking pace. For half a lap the mare goes on a loose rein, stretches, snorts, then Judith pulls more tightly on the reins again, gallops and jumps. Pure happiness. Each time. Utterly reliable.

Later, back home, she makes some herbal tea, brushes her teeth, gets undressed, and takes the pot of tea to bed with her. She sends a good night message to G.H.—known to her now as Gregor—he writes back immediately, then she reads a few pages of a new Bach biography, drinks her tea, closes the book, turns out the light, and falls asleep within minutes.

Judith has been sleeping better since she hooked up with Gregor.

It was astonishingly easy. They met at the Bach statue by the Thomaskirche, then wandered into the dusk and had dinner at a Japanese restaurant. They talked for a good three hours. First about work, then their interests, and finally about their expectations from a relationship. The tone was business-like. As if love were a contractual item, they checked the individual paragraphs for pitfalls, they negotiated, and came to an agreement.

He wasn't interested in a fling. What he was looking for was a companion, an intellectual counterpart. He wanted dependability paired with cerebral and physical intimacy, although the latter seemed to be slightly less important to him than mental and emotional attachment. He could imagine living together, though that wasn't absolutely necessary and certainly not at any price. Faithfulness was important, but he said he was prepared to tolerate a discreet affair if his sexual potency waned.

On neither of their first two meetings did he display that male drive which Judith both needed but which also repulsed her. He wooed her without applying any pressure. His calm, intelligent manner didn't arouse any extravagant feelings in her. The symptoms of being in love failed to materialize at all.

When they met he would kiss her on the cheek and ask about her day, fixing his gray-green eyes on her. Occasionally his elegantly curved lips displayed an ironic smile and from time to time he would run a hand through his short gray hair. It was the symmetry that Judith liked. Nothing about Gregor's face was jarring.

She liked gazing at him. She liked listening to him. When he invited her to one of his trials she went along. The chamber in which he was the presiding judge was ruling on asylum petitions and subsidiary protection for people from the Maghreb countries, Syria, and the Balkan states. They were taking legal action against those authorities who had rejected their applications.

I swear that I will translate faithfully and conscientiously. While the interpreter read the oath, Gregor smiled at her again. Then he focused only on the claimants, the interpreter, and the bored-looking lawyer.

Gregor's knowledge about the current situation was extensive, and every day more files would arrive with expert witness reports. He and his colleagues were the court of first instance.

Their rulings could be challenged. But even if they were confirmed by all courts, deportations were rarely carried out. Meticulous, painstaking work often came to nothing.

He was likewise calm when talking about himself and the past. His two children were grown up, his ex-wife had recently begun a new relationship, and he had been alone for the past three years since the divorce.

They took lengthy walks, went to concerts and restaurants. Gregor paid, held the door open for her, helped her out of her coat and back into it. He was so obviously from a different time that Judith had to stop herself from making any comments to this effect.

It was a whole month before they first slept together. For Gregor the decision was made that night. His face, when he looked at her, wasn't just marked by interest, but certainty, too.

The sex hadn't been anything special. Occasionally she'd thought of Hans and the way his hands made her body tingle. While Gregor was moving in and out of her she wanted to ask him to dispense with his politeness in bed. But he took a condom out from under the pillow, and when Judith explained what he had to do to ensure she climaxed, too, it was already over. Later he attended to her desire, then rolled over beside her, lay on his side, pulled her toward him, and tenderly kissed the back of her neck.

Judith fell asleep. And when she awoke, she was still in his arms. Three hours had passed, three hours in which he hadn't let go of her.

*

The sensitivity has lasted for three days now. Even the white material of her nightshirt is painful when it slides over her breasts.

She sits on the toilet, holds the toothbrush mug beneath her, and pees into it.

Two blue lines.

She empties the toothbrush mug into the toilet bowl, throws the test into the bin, and drives to the practice where, with a curt greeting and avoiding eye contact, she crosses the waiting room and breezily shuts the door of consultation room 1 behind her.

At the end of morning appointments she loses her patience. She cuts short an elderly woman who is going to great lengths to describe her illness. Without beating about the bush she tells this hypochondriac, who turns up several times a month, that she should see a psychotherapist.

For lunch she has spicy coconut soup with tofu in a Thai fast-food restaurant. In the window is a rubber plant with flashing fairy lights and a plastic Father Christmas. As she waits for her food to be called she observes the other people. Every single one of them is tapping on their smartphone. Judith gets her mobile out of her bag too. She writes Gregor a message, but doesn't send it.

She knows when it happened.

That day, around three and a half weeks ago, Gregor didn't

get in touch at all, which was unlike him. The hours at the office seemed to drag on forever. They were due to meet in the evening, but the evening was far off. At around 2 p.m. she wished her colleagues a nice weekend, plucked a parking ticket from beneath the right-hand windshield wiper, tossed it onto the passenger seat with the other parking tickets, drove home, and got changed.

She ran her distance of five miles in record time, and without glancing at her phone once. Back home she jumped into the shower and then checked her mobile every minute, the screen fogging up with steam. She wiped the mirror with toilet paper, put on mascara and lipstick, and smelled her own fear.

His silence tormented her, eating into her insides and making her hands tremble. A man who could put her vegetative nervous system out of balance was dangerous. She tried in vain to persuade herself that there was nothing to worry about. The body was smarter than the mind.

Gregor greeted her with a friendly reserve. A brief peck on the cheek was the only physical contact. He avoided her gaze and something in his expression was different. He looked grayer, as if the aging process had taken a leap forward. She felt her hands start to shake and cold sweat covered her palms.

Judith couldn't eat a single mouthful, and when Gregor got up to clear her plate away, she took it from him and put it back on the table.

He sat down again.

Then he asked whether she was actually interested in him or whether she was merely try to deal with her own loneliness.

Fucking and culture, Gregor went on, wasn't what he was after. Then he repeated the words and it seemed he realized he'd hit the bull's-eye only after he uttered them.

Fucking and culture, fucking and culture.

He told her about his day.

In the morning he'd found his tires slashed and was late for work for the very first time.

In the afternoon his clever questioning exposed the story of a Libyan's flight as a lie. The man knew the game was over. He got up, pushed away the arm of his lawyer, who was trying to placate him, and launched into a tirade. Instead of calling him to order, Gregor instructed the interpreter to translate.

He hurled abuse at Germany, predicting the country's downfall.

When Gregor returned to his office and took off his robes, he was exhausted.

I need something nice, he told Judith, *something to make me feel better.*

It must have happened that night.

Judith eats her soup and peers out of the window of the restaurant. Sleet, wind, hunched people with hooded faces. Barely any cyclists, but convoys of cars and the air so thick you could cut it with a knife. The spiciness of the soup brings tears to her eyes.

She puts on her coat, gets into the car, which she parked illegally right outside, puts on *Winterreise*, and drives to a house visit in eastern Leipzig.

Woman, sixty-eight, living on her own.

Judith switches off the television and empties the overflowing ashtray. She opens the window and examines the woman's legs. *This is the third incidence of phlebitis in half a year*, she says in the tone that some patients need to understand the seriousness of the situation. *I'm going to have you admitted to hospital as the risk of thrombosis is just too high.*

The ambulance arrives swiftly. As the paramedics link arms with the protesting woman and lead her down the stairs, Judith writes Gregor another message. *I have to see you. I'm pregnant.* She steps outside, pulls the zip of her coat right to the top and the fur hood over her head, reads the message again, and sends it to Paula.

✳

Paula opens the door in trainers and running gear, her cheeks red. Leni is sitting at the kitchen table cutting cookies from rolled-out dough. Since Paula started running regularly her state has dramatically improved.

We can talk in a minute, she says. *Just let me have a quick shower.*

Judith sits with Leni. Together they cut out Christmas trees, bells, hearts, and stars. Leni asks about the horse and when she can go riding again. Judith promises to take her along the next time she goes.

When Paula appears in her dressing gown and a turban towel, strokes Leni's hair, and gives her a kiss on the forehead, Judith looks away.

Paula puts the baking tray with the cookies in the oven, sets the timer, then sends Leni to her room.

Judith ought to have known that Paula wouldn't offer neutral advice in this matter. Before Leni was born she got the nesting instinct in textbook fashion. Then, after the birth, she, Ludger, and the baby cocooned themselves. For months they lived only in symbiotic unity.

It will change you, she says, *you'll have worries you never knew existed before, feel pain that's deeper than any other pain.*

All the same she advises Judith to have the child.

Does Gregor know? she asks.

Judith shakes her head.

Aren't you going to tell him?

No, I don't want to, Judith replies tetchily.

She gets up and looks out of the window.

The apartment in the building opposite is brightly lit. A child is sitting on a swing hanging in the doorway between two rooms. It appears in one window, disappears for a moment, then reappears in the other. The child swings so high that it looks as if it might hit its head on the ceiling at any moment. In the room to the left is the mother, in the one to the right the father. Both appear delighted by the wild swinging.

Judith tries in vain to see herself as a mother. She cannot picture herself with a child. And because there's no picture, there'll be no child.

Will you pick me up after the procedure? she asks.

Paula nods hesitantly, and outside it begins to snow.

＊

It is not quite 8 a.m. when Judith arrives at the clinic with her overnight bag. She hasn't eaten anything for twelve hours. The clinic is in the basement of a residential house. She and a group of other women are taken to the operating ward and divided up between three rooms. They are told to get undressed, lie in bed, and wait for the anesthetist.

Not all the women are here for the same reason.

Some are having cervical polyps removed, tissue samples taken from the mucous membrane of the uterus, or uterine abrasion to stop excessive bleeding. Separated from the invalids, Judith and two other women are in a connecting room. She's not imagining it—the nurse is having a friendly chat in the next-door room, but to them she just gave terse, clear instructions: don't eat anything, don't drink anything, switch off your phone, wait for the anesthetist.

Judith looks around. Christmas decorations hang in the window, homemade origami stars. The two other women are lying quietly in their beds. They've turned to the wall and secretly switched their mobiles back on. Both are young. One is overweight, the other slim but nondescript.

Judith knows what to expect. Lie and wait. Listen for footsteps, keep an eye on the doors, calm the thoughts spinning around your head.

It's not her first time.

If she'd managed to have her way when she was eighteen and ignored her mother, Judith would have a grown-up child now.

Presumably it would be sporty and good-looking, just as she and her PE teacher were. But her mother painted such a bleak picture of her professional future that Judith eventually agreed to the abortion.

Something is happening in the neighboring room. The innocents are being seen to first. Brisk footsteps cross the room, a male voice speaks to the first patient. A last piece of advice, a joke that isn't funny.

Where does she know that voice from?

It's now fourteen hours since she last ate. She's finding it hard to think clearly. This is her third abortion; the second was after sleeping with a man she barely knew. There is every indication that here and now she is giving up her last chance of having a child. Soon she'll be too old; past forty the rate of spontaneous pregnancy is only two percent. Of one hundred women who have unprotected sex, two will get pregnant. It's unlikely she'd be one of those two women.

She could get up, get dressed, and go.

She could call Paula and tell her to come and fetch her. They'd spend the day together drawing up a list of names.

Judith takes her phone from the bag beside her bed. Gregor and Paula were the last to call. Gregor rang yesterday evening from Berlin, where he was giving a lecture at a conference. He'd be staying on for another day to see his eldest daughter. By the time he returned she would be in good enough shape to keep the intervention secret from him. The abortion itself takes no more than a quarter of an hour; facemask anesthesia doesn't require artificial ventilation. She would wake up, recover in a few hours, and sleep in her own bed tonight, as if nothing had happened.

One last time she allows herself to think about what it would be like to keep the child. For the first year she could organize a replacement at the office, and after that she would take on a nanny. They would have the money for this. If she rang him now and told him everything . . .

The mobile is still in her hand.

✳ ✳ ✳

Ten days ago she came back from a riding vacation in Montana. Nobody picked her up from the airport.

For the past ten days she's been trying in vain to find pleasure in normal things.

The nights are endless. Getting to sleep isn't a problem, but she wakes up after a couple of hours. The contours of her body seem to be disintegrating. Her hands and feet feel very distant. Proportions are shifting. It's as if invisible beings are pulling at her limbs, and only her head is in its place on the pillow. She doesn't feel any pain, just a faint tingling.

The more awake she is, the more her body comes back together again. And then the image appears. Every night.

Before her lies a heap consisting of everything her body has lost to date: hair, shed skin, fingernails, toenails, snot, mucus, blood, sweat, feces, and urine. It's a stinking, sticky mountain of organic material, and she can't stop thinking that the other seven billion people on earth have piles like this too. She tosses and turns, takes deep breaths through her nose and breathes out again through her mouth. Reaches for the water glass beside the bed, drinks, and doesn't dare glance at the clock.

At some point early in the morning, sleep returns. The dreams it brings are as dark as the thoughts preceding it. It's only the noise of the alarm that releases her from the strains of the night.

Judith arrived at work tired again today, but still went riding in the afternoon—without saddle or snaffle, just with a rope and halter.

She makes a salad, then logs onto the site and looks at the latest dating suggestions. She doesn't want to spend her next birthday alone.

Entrepreneur, 45, two children, neither at home, casual smoker and cat owner, has sent a smile. His response to the question of who he'd like to meet is: Me in ten years' time.

She scrolls down. What I'm allergic to: Body hair (apart from on the head). Judith clicks to get rid of him and keeps looking.

Architect, 48, no pets, no children, no desire to have children. His personal quotation is from Hemingway rather than himself, but at least he makes no mention of body hair.

She gave up looking for almost two years, hoping for a chance meeting, and she even contemplated being on her own permanently. She had her work, her horse, and her friends—Paula and Brida. There was no room for a man. It was only when Paula rang to tell her about Wenzel that Judith became aware again of how difficult it is to be alone.

She goes into the kitchen, pours herself a glass of red wine, and checks the time. In an hour she needs to be at the bookshop. Brida is reading from her new novel.

Wenzel will be there too. When Paula introduced him, Judith was almost lost for words. Wenzel Goldfuss had barely changed since that day several years ago when, on one of her house calls, Judith visited his cancer-ridden wife, Maja, and then left their lovely apartment with a curious sense of envy. His wife was long dead and life had gone on. It had brought Paula and him together, and driven Judith and Gregor apart.

Brida would call it fate.

But Judith doesn't believe in fate. What people call fate is nothing more than the sum of the decisions they make.

She's craving a cigarette, but she's given up smoking. She goes back to the computer and clicks open the next profile.

Engineer, 45, divorced, nonsmoker, two children, none at home, likes rock, pop, and easy listening, and is looking for a nice woman he can make happy.

She closes the laptop in resignation.

She didn't meet another man like Gregor. They still bump into each other occasionally, and they'll say a polite hello without stopping.

The child would be two and a half now. Back then in the day clinic, shortly before the abortion, there was a tiny chance it might have lived. But then the door opened, the anesthetist came into the room, and Judith realized where she knew the voice from.

So we meet again, he muttered, lowering his gaze. As he filled out the anesthesia form she couldn't help imagining Doctor,

45, with his own horse, naked. Shackled, on all fours, with lash marks on his back.

They didn't look each other in the eye. Later, on the way to the operating theater, Sven wished her all the best and a happy Christmas. Then the bright lights blurred, the voices faded, and she fell asleep. When she awoke, her pregnancy had been terminated.

Back from the conference in Berlin, Gregor appeared at her door with a bunch of white roses. It came out of her like a contaminated meal. She practically vomited it at his feet.

Gregor slowly repeated what she had said. She'd been pregnant with his child, but had an abortion, which meant the problem was solved and they ought to be more careful in the future.

As so often, it was only when he repeated them out loud that things seemed to acquire some order in his head and their significance become apparent. During the ensuing silence he must have made his decision. Judith had seen the change in his expression. Even before he said another word, she knew she'd be spending Christmas alone. It was the day before the winter solstice, with fewer than eight hours separating the rising and setting of the sun. She left the house in the dark and in the dark she returned. When Gregor went, she knew she'd miss him terribly.

The roses reminded her of him daily, and as if that weren't enough, they didn't wilt. They lasted through Christmas and were still standing upright in the vase on New Year's Eve, with just the edges of the petals browning.

On Christmas Eve, as soon as she got out of bed, Judith

sent Gregor a conciliatory message, but she didn't receive an answer. So she went to see the horse and rode for a good two hours along muddy forest paths, then prepared a bucketful of feed pellets and watched the mare greedily demolish her festive treat. In the afternoon she opened a bottle of wine and began a television marathon. When the doorbell rang early that evening, she couldn't help but hope.

Judith wandered slowly to the door, lifted the receiver of the intercom, whispered a timid *Hello*, and waited. But instead of Gregor's serene bass she heard a high-pitched child's voice wishing her Merry Christmas. The disappointment paralyzed her for several seconds. She made herself breathe deeply and calmly, then she went to the window, leaned out and saw her neighbors streaming out of the buildings. As every year, a small delegation from the Thomaner choir had come to the street, around ten boys who now started singing "Silent Night" with pure clarity.

Judith lit a cigarette. Cold air came pouring into her un-decorated room. The boys sang the next song, *"Es ist ein Ros' entsprungen,"* in several parts.

She gently closed the window and resumed her series on the television.

Since then so little has happened that the last few years seem like days. Only her trips to the stables have interrupted the never-changing rhythm of work and exercise, expanding the time to an extent that didn't correspond to what had actually passed, but it did allow for memory.

She carefully applies makeup, puts Brida's new book in her

bag, walks through a thick snow flurry for fifteen minutes, and wishes she didn't have to enter the bookshop alone.

She could have asked Hans, but things have become awkward because the short, thin wife found out something, and since then Hans has made himself scarce.

She needs to hurry if she doesn't want to be late. Snowflakes stick to her eyelashes and as she walks Judith thinks of her childhood winters in the Ore Mountains. Scratchy tights, hand-knitted scarves and hats. Her mother goose-stepping up front, Judith and her father behind, onward and upward through forests thickly covered with snow, until the trees became shorter, grew more sparsely, and were angled in one direction by the wind. They stood there like crooked sculptures, surrounded by ice and snow. Then the picnic in a wind-sheltered spot: sandwiches, tea, chocolate, nuts, and sometimes a helping of praise from her mother. For Judith did not complain. Neither about the cold nor her sodden boots or half-frozen limbs. Nor about the length of the walk nor the constantly high tempo, which was always quicker than a child's.

Judith strides rapidly now, too, just as she did back then. She gets to the bookshop on time, takes off her coat and scarf, pats the thawing snow from her eyelashes, and looks around. Most of the seats have been taken.

Paula and Wenzel wave at her from the front row, while farther back somebody turns to her.

The seat next to Gregor is free. She sits down, says hello, then the lights dim and Brida begins to read. From the corner of her eye Judith can see his head turning in her direction.

PART THREE

Brida

A stag emerges from the forest.

He steps forward, looks around, and begins to graze, suspecting nothing. From time to time the stag raises his head, looks from side to side, then continues to graze.

About one hundred and fifty yards separates the raised hunting stand from the stag, a stretch of uncultivated land—a wild, overgrown meadow from which the occasional bird flies up.

Brida lowers the binoculars and picks up an imaginary rifle. She aims, shoots, and hits the stag. Then she bends forward, leaning against the cracked rail. The old wood crunches. Insects have eaten their way into it. In the corners of the stand are large spiders' webs full of prey.

Her legs shudder as rough hands move up the insides of her thighs. Götz pushes up her skirt. She raises her head and looks across the meadow at the setting sun. The stag turns and disappears into the forest.

She closes her eyes.

They take the winding path through the hills back to the vacation cottages.

Crickets are chirping and twice they come across a slow-worm. Götz holds her hand and sets the pace. When they reach the sign for Hollershagen, he lets go of her hand. He points up at the sky. A flock of cranes flies overhead. A corner of her panties protrudes from the right-hand pocket of his windbreaker. For a moment Brida fantasizes about leaving them there. Svenja would find them and then . . .

What then?

The thought of the children makes her reach for her panties and pull them out.

The girls come running toward them. She and Götz brought the children up together for four years, then Brida left him.

A renewed attempt gave them another year of family life. Now Hermine and Undine are eleven and nine, and Götz and Svenja have been a couple for more than two years.

✳

Before Svenja appeared on the scene, Brida had seen their separation merely as a change in the status of their relationship. Although she and Götz no longer lived together and didn't share their daily lives, they still had sex and she always felt that one clear sign would be all that was needed for a fresh start.

They agreed on the bird-nesting model, whereby the children stay in the apartment and the parents take turns living there. When Brida stayed with the girls, Götz would sleep in the workshop, whereas Brida had a room in a flat-share when she was not with the children.

They discussed the children's issues very reasonably. They celebrated Christmas and Easter and went on vacation together.

The desire for a clean break didn't come from her.

One day when Götz was moving back into the apartment and Brida was packing up her stuff, he asked her to stay for a while. They had dinner together with the children and she still remembers what they ate: green salad with tomatoes and toasted pine nuts, vegan spaghetti carbonara, and homemade chocolate mousse for dessert. Throughout the meal he avoided her gaze, and when the children got up from the table and rushed to their rooms, he stood up, too, and followed them.

Only later, when they were asleep, did he get to the point. *We ought to think about getting a divorce*, he said, adding softly, *but it doesn't have to be immediately.*

✳

Not long after she saw the two of them in town.

They were standing outside a café, Svenja in a miniskirt and tall boots, Götz in jeans and a sweater Brida had never seen before. Svenja was looking up at him. She was short and delicate, and despite her high heels only came up to his shoulders. Her head was tilted so that the tip of her ponytail touched her back. She smiled and ran her right index finger across his chest.

Brida was unable to take another step. The pain hit her coldly and unexpectedly. She gripped the handlebars of her bike and stared over at them.

Until then they had conducted their affairs openly, even telling each other about them and making comparisons. But no other woman or man really had a chance. And so new partners went as they had come—inconspicuous, and ultimately insignificant. This time, however, Brida had been totally unaware.

When he cradled the other woman's head in his hands, bent, and gave her a lengthy kiss, Brida couldn't look away. And as he smiled, took her hand, and they went into the café, Brida kept staring. Then they were inside, out of sight.

When her legs began to obey her again, she wheeled her bicycle around the next corner and rang Judith.

At Dr. Gabriel's office nobody answered. It was a Wednesday afternoon. Judith's mobile was switched off, too; she was probably with her horse.

Brida picked up the children. She dragged herself up the stairs to the apartment, made it into the sitting room, and slumped onto the sofa. Her fears were justified. She knew. And when Judith eventually called back, she said at once, *He's got another woman and this time it's serious.*

If she ever comes to Hollershagen again, it will be without Svenja.

Götz and the girls go into number 7. Brida unlocks the door to number 8. She's spending vacations wall to wall with his new girlfriend, and Judith's words from that telephone call echo in her head.

You only want him back because you can't have him anymore.
When he drops the other woman you won't want him anymore.
You don't need him.
You'll get by on your own.

To the rear of the cottages, facing west, are the terraces,

separated by shoulder-height hedges. Unless you whisper, every word inevitably drifts over to the neighbors.

Brida stands on her terrace, smoking. The wind blows the smoke next door, where Svenja and Götz are sitting outside. They're discussing the day ahead, comparing the prices of boat rentals and planning the route they're going to canoe with the children.

There's a splinter in Brida's left hand from the wooden hunting stand. She fetches a pair of tweezers from the bathroom, extracts the splinter, and flicks it over the hedge.

*

Over dinner she watches Svenja. There is not a trace of uncertainty in the woman's face. Half disgusted, half fascinated, Brida gazes at the victor. She won him over with her younger body that hasn't borne any children, hasn't suffered a serious illness, hasn't had a crisis, a body that knows only exercise and healthy food. And with her fresh mind, which isn't too deep or too shallow. Svenja is so sure of herself that when the children said they wanted to spend the vacation with both parents, she agreed.

Brida can't look at Svenja anymore, so she turns her attention to Götz. He's jiggling his right foot, avoiding eye contact.

When Svenja and the girls go to the buffet for seconds, he says quietly:

This is a mistake.

What exactly is the mistake? she asks.

You know, he whispers.

Later he plays volleyball with Svenja, the girls, and a few other vacation guests. Svenja makes up for her lack of height with persistence and a willingness to take risks. She throws herself onto the sand, leaps back to her feet, jumps, runs, and belts the ball powerfully over the net. Hermine tries to emulate her, Undine gets in the way.

Brida isn't any good at ball games either. As a child she used to duck whenever a ball came her way. She would forever be injuring herself and nobody wanted her on their team. She walks back to the cottage, fetches water bottles, and mosquito spray for the girls, then carries on to the bathing jetty and gazes out at the lake for a while.

From a nearby pasture she can hear cattle lowing. They've been lowing for days.

She'd like to tell Götz, ask him to go and see the farmer with her. But she doesn't follow her impulse. He's no longer the person she relates to. He's no longer her husband. She has to say it. Again and again.

He's no longer my husband.

✳ ✳ ✳

Brida knew at once that Götz would become her husband.

She'd been living in Leipzig for a while, but the apartment wasn't yet furnished. When she entered his shop a bell rang. For a while she was alone with the pieces of restored antique furniture. The prices were written by hand on slips of paper and discreetly displayed. Her favorite piece was a child's bed. The head and foot were painted with flowers, the colors touched up only in parts. They were alpine flowers: gentian and edelweiss. Brida sat carefully on the edge of the bed, and although she wasn't certain she wanted a child, she considered buying it.

She heard footsteps and then he was standing beside her.

He dried his hands on dirty trousers and greeted her with the words, *I'm afraid the bed isn't for sale.*

At that moment it became dark. There was a downpour and hailstones hammered against the shop window. Brida stood up.

That's what happens when I'm angry, you see, she said, without a hint of irony in her voice.

He peered at the storm outside and then looked back at her. It was as if he believed in her power. But then he began to smile, almost imperceptibly. First with his eyes, which narrowed slightly, then it spread to his lips.

Brida felt it in every fiber of her body. Something took hold of her. The rhythm of her heart went out of control. She stood very still. Her hands were bathed in sweat. Hail crashed against the window, the door flew open, and the bell rang out wildly.

Two other customers entered the shop.

The magical moment had passed.

While he offered the soaked couple some coffee and sold them a pair of Thonet café chairs, she took a snoop around. Later she followed him into the workshop.

A cupboard stood on a large piece of cardboard. It was varnished a natural white with two glass doors and four shelves and was exactly what she'd been looking for. Götz explained the provenance of the cupboard as if he were recounting someone's biography—installed in the chemistry lab of a village school in Saxony in the 1920s, for the next ninety years it had been a silent witness to the building's changing history. At the end of the war the school was turned into a home for refugees, then became a school again, after which it was a teacher training center before finishing up as a youth hostel.

Most of the old furniture had been unsalvageable, either rotten or devoured by woodworm. All apart from this cupboard, which stood alone in a small, warm, south-facing room, covered and preserved. When Götz found it, it contained an assortment of test tubes and glass bulbs.

He ran his hand over the wood and named a price that was anything but modest. Brida said yes without hesitating.

As they went back to the desk in the salesroom to discuss transport, the rain stopped as abruptly as it had begun. Now the sun was shining brightly and the room shone. Götz asked Brida for her surname and laughed, shaking his head, when he heard the answer. Brida repeated it.

Brida Lichtblau? he asked, looking pointedly at the crisp blue sky outside.

Yes, she said. *Lichtblau, like light and blue.*

He wrote down the name, putting an exclamation mark after it.

*

Götz delivered the cupboard himself.

He carried it in sections up to the third floor. Each of the sections was marked in pencil to show where it went. The back and the sides slotted together; the entire piece could be assembled without screws or nails. After half an hour it stood there, finished.

While Götz washed his hands in the bathroom, Brida made some coffee.

It was summer, so they sat on the balcony, looking out over the green inner courtyard, and heard the voices of children playing below. He asked her what she did and she said, *I'm going to become a writer.*

He took a cigarette from the little breast pocket of his shirt and a lighter from his trouser pocket. *Is that something you can become?* he asked.

She was confused by his question.

I'm sorry, he added, *I didn't mean to be impolite.*

Patches of sweat had formed in his armpits. His gaze was fixed on her. Brida felt as if those eyes were boring right into her head, penetrating every coil of her brain, to the very center of her ego.

Instead of answering his question she talked about her childhood in Mecklenburg, her training as a hunter, the four semesters of forestry she studied in a small town near Dresden, and how unexpectedly she had won a place at the German Institute for Literature. She'd abandoned her forestry studies, given notice on her rented room, and moved to Leipzig.

The story Brida submitted had simply flowed out of her after she'd sat down one morning and launched into it. She was caught by a surge that drove her along and at some point, days later, washed her back up onshore together with the finished story.

That's what I mean, Götz said. *That's exactly what I mean.*

When he got up to go, she accompanied him to the stairwell.

As he said good-bye they stared into each other's eyes. His handshake was warm and firm, and then he pushed her back across the threshold into her apartment, closed the door, and kissed her.

* * *

Brida left home at the age of nineteen, intact. Now, almost twenty years later, she feels as if all her bones were suddenly broken, her skin ripped from her body, her hair torn out, her confidence stolen, and her dreams shattered. She no longer has anything in common with the person she once was.

The months of breastfeeding have turned her breasts into empty shells, the sleepless nights have drawn shadows across her face and the tears have hollowed it out.

She knows more than she did back then, but what use is this to her?

She ought to have known *back then*. When she met Götz. When she was young and able to write. The wisdom of age seems to be worthless. Younger people aren't interested in it and the elderly are too old to be able to make anything of it.

She sits in the dining room of the manor house, looking at the other families, the whining little children, the sullen teenagers. Her own children are still asleep and there's no sign of

Götz or Svenja. She can't eat anything. All she can stomach is coffee.

Brida hasn't written anything for months. Her last attempt resulted in sentences without tension, without any tone, without magic.

Her body has lost its tension, too, as if it had forgotten its potential. With the divorce Götz extinguished Brida's desire. With every meeting he stokes it again, and with every parting he puts it out once more. She both loves and hates him for this.

Then she spots him by the coffee machine. On his own. He turns to her and smiles.

*

Around noon they get into the car to fetch some pizza. The children are lying by the lake, reading. Svenja is at a yoga session. Once out of the resort, Götz turns onto a forest path. He parks the transporter well hidden among some trees and then lays out a blanket in the cargo area.

Brida weeps.

We don't have to, he says softly.

But Brida does have to.

Later she asks what keeps him together with Svenja.

She's harmless, he says. *She's got a talent for being happy. Do you understand what I mean when I say she's in the world?* She can hear him breathing in and out. *I'm exhausted, Brida, I need an easy life. I need a laugh in the evenings.*

What else? she asks.

He hesitates. *Can you cope with the answers to your questions?*
She nods.

Then he says nothing for a while. Brida knows he's not trying
to avoid answering. He's economical and precise with his words.

Svenja, he finally begins, *doesn't take herself seriously. She's
supportive of me, even when it means putting her own needs
second.*

Didn't I do that too?

*Yes, of course, but you found it hard. You suffered with it. And
because you suffered, the children and I weren't happy either.*

Brida doesn't want to cry now. With her breathing she con-
trols the pain, the tears, and also the objections. These were just
a lie, anyway; everything Götz is saying is true. And because
it's true, hope has become pointless. For Brida is still Brida
and Götz is still Götz. His arms are tightly wrapped around
her when he casually mentions that Svenja wants a baby. Brida
wriggles from his grasp and sits up.

Don't do it, she says.

Maybe it's a good thing, Brida, he replies. *I mean, we have to
live our lives. Without each other.*

Is that what you want? she asks.

No, he says, *it's got nothing to do with wanting.*

He takes her hand and puts it up to his cheek.

Do you love her?

*I like her a lot. If I loved her, I wouldn't have an easy life. It
would be like it is between us.*

Brida takes a deep breath. Every question is dangerous. Every answer could be one too many.

How is it between us? she asks.

He looks at his watch. *We were going to get some pizza,* he mutters. *They'll be waiting.*

Götz, how is it between us?

He rubs his face before he speaks.

Do you remember telling the girls that you didn't know what got into you when you decided to have children rather than write? Do you remember the look on their faces?

Yes, she remembers. Hermine took her little sister's hand and dragged her into their room, where they built a barricade. Through the door Brida apologized and swore she hadn't meant it that way, she'd always wanted children and was happy every day she spent with them.

And she meant what she said, even though they had destroyed her text. Months of work had been deleted, obliterated, forever. She wept and cursed and said things that would have been better left unsaid.

She remembers the rest of the day too. The aggressive symbiosis of father and daughters. The front erected against her. Brida didn't know what to say. Later she crept silently past the open door to the children's room and heard his reading voice uttering words from a safe children's world.

The wine in the kitchen had been drunk too quickly and she smoked a cigarette inside, at the kitchen table, going against what they'd agreed.

It's not the girls' fault! You should have made backup copies, Brida!

He had walked past her, thrown the window open, and hurled these words in her face.

And you've got to teach the children! They shouldn't be fiddling with my computer! she'd yelled, and gone on drinking.

Of course she remembers.

But he ought to remember other things.

She puts her hand on his chest, runs it down over his belly button, and clasps his penis. Then she slides down him and lies her head on his warm stomach.

As Brida and Götz are carrying the pizza boxes from the car to their accommodation, Svenja comes out to meet them. *You took your time,* she says. *We've been waiting for ages.*

Brida looks Svenja in the eye and smiles.

✳ ✳ ✳

At the beginning of their relationship there was Malika, who Götz said at the time was the woman to start a family with. Her body was a mother's body—soft and warm, like a protective winter coat. *What am I like, then?* she asked him, and Götz said, *Wild and rough, like a cat's tongue.* Brida laughed, kissed Götz, and told him about Johann, the poet, her boyfriend.

Thinking about Johann and Malika doesn't make her feel at all guilty.

Brida believes fervently that love comes as it should come— unprovoked, blamelessly and compellingly. It can't be controlled and can't be stopped. Any attempt to rebel against it is a pointless waste of time and effort.

Johann accepted their separation silently, but he never said another word to her.

Malika, on the other hand, remained on the scene.

*

To begin with they met mostly at her place, and occasionally in one of the rooms off the workshop. She accompanied him as often as she could on his trips to the east. His search for antique furniture took him mainly to Poland and the Czech Republic. It was only on these trips that Brida could touch him whenever and wherever it took her fancy. While Malika gave violin lessons back at home, Brida had him all to herself.

They would tell each other their sexual fantasies on deserted country roads. Then they would turn off into the forest, stop in secluded places, and in the back of the van do those things which became the yardstick for their relationship.

It was after those trips that she wrote her first longish stories, inspired by the places they'd visited.

A run-down estate in rural Poland was the setting for a drama about two children, while a Czech farm was the starting point for a novella.

Götz climbed up into a number of attics and elbowed his way through barns crammed with stuff. Like a hunter he would wait calmly and patiently for the right moment. He took his time to get in contact with people, and if there could be no verbal agreement because of the language barrier, then he would get by with simple gestures. He often wandered around silently, touching the things he saw, or just stopped and stared.

People trusted him. They allowed him into their storerooms, attics, barns, garages, and homes, and just as the sculptor can often see the figure in the block of stone, so Götz could see the future ornament in unremarkable furniture. And, always anxious not to cheat people, he would rather pay too much than too little.

Brida, too, felt totally assured in his company. But as soon as the journey home began and they got closer to Germany, the more distant Götz became. Back home, he would drop her off outside her apartment and drive on to the workshop, which represented the boundary between Malika and her.

It might be days before she heard from him again.

She kept to herself at the Institute.

It wasn't that she'd made a particular effort to form friendships before she met Götz, but she had certainly taken part in student life. She turned up to parties and went regularly to the cinema with Alma and Xandrine, who wrote prose texts too. Usually, however, she preferred the company of a good book. Brida strictly avoided large gatherings such as New Year's Eve celebrations, rock concerts, and neighborhood festivities. It had always given her a curious pleasure to not be present when everyone came together.

Being on her own had always been her natural state. As a solitary child in a solitary house on the edge of the forest, she'd had no choice other than to organize her time herself. Her mother left the house early in the morning and came back late. Every day she spent two hours commuting by bike, then train and on foot to work at the savings bank in the nearest town. Her father spent most of the time in the forest, where he was responsible for a large area. Brida accompanied him sometimes, though often she stayed on her own in the house with its big garden and the tall surrounding fence.

Only rarely did another child from the village come to the forester's house. It was far away and people thought that Brida was odd. Janko, a male hunting dog, followed her wherever she went. Although occasionally she longed for playmates and begged her mother for a little brother or sister, she couldn't put up with the company of another child for very long. After an hour or two at most she would have had enough. Either she would stop talking or become mean, driven on by an unbearable tension inside her.

Once she just left. Summoning Janko with a whistle, she disappeared with him into the forest, deserting her visitor in the garden.

The apology she later gave under pressure from her parents was so halfhearted that there was no proper reconciliation, and the child never visited again.

Brida couldn't have cared less. She was able to make her own entertainment. All she needed was her head. Any random thought was enough to bring forth a stream of images and feelings. And when she got to the age where ideas were no longer games, she began to write down the characters and places from her inner world, which meant she needed more than ever to be alone. She cultivated it, shielding herself from intrusion by a reality that could never be as intense as the cosmos of her imagination.

Now her life consisted of Götz and writing, and finally she really did have something to say.

Like those of many of her fellow students, Brida's stories lacked experience. Most of the students were young, their first literary efforts the product of a protected childhood and banal infatuations. The lack of human understanding and worldly wisdom led to overconstructed, unbelievable characters and plots. The texts that focused on style alone were of no interest to anyone outside the Institute.

Being Götz's lover was a gift.

Brida plunged as deeply as she could into humiliation, longing, and anxiety. Dozens of pages of text appeared over the course of sleepless nights in which she waited in vain for a sign from him. His presence was the nourishment that sustained her during their next separation.

But the time spent with him was always too brief, and the intervals between their encounters too long.

For almost a year her body sent out its warning signals at ever decreasing intervals. One illness would give way to another, and after every possible cause was ruled out save for Malika, she asked him to leave her.

His answer was no. He would only break up with Malika if the decision came from the heart. If he merely did it to satisfy Brida's wishes, it would be worthless.

When she asked him if her loved her, he said yes without hesitation.

When she asked if he loved Malika, he gave the same answer.

The weeks and months then flowed indistinguishably into one another. The pain colored her writing. It generated too much pathos, created too many metaphors, and constructed too many adjectives in her prose.

Brida's fellow students picked her writing to pieces in seminars, while her tutors made no secret of the fact that they considered her study at the Institute to be a mistake. Nobody, not even her parents, had ever taken seriously her idea of becoming a writer. Götz was the only one who believed in her.

More months passed.

A scaly rash appeared around her mouth, her hair became dull, and every smile involved a disproportionate effort. The summer semester was almost at an end, the swifts chased through the streets at night, and the lime blossom gave off its sweet fragrance.

One evening Götz sat fully dressed on the edge of the bed, gazing out of the window. Malika was expecting him. His phone had already vibrated several times. On each occasion his fingers had twitched. Brida had remained apprehensively silent.

I ought to tell Malika, he said eventually, lowering his head.

Brida didn't understand straightaway. She lay there before him, naked and still.

Maybe she'll understand, he added softly.

What about me? she said, abruptly sitting up.

I don't know, he said. Götz put the phone in his pocket and left.

The following day, nothing existed for Brida save her innermost pain. All external phenomena simply rebounded off her.

That morning's poetry seminar reached her ears but not her brain. The lecturer stood at the front of the group, opening and closing her mouth. Sounds poured from the other students' mouths. Nothing made any sense.

In aesthetic, cultural, and linguistic theory the concepts blurred, swelled, and disgorged meaninglessly into the room.

She couldn't cope with the novel seminar in the afternoon. In the middle of the session she got up, left the room without closing the door, ran down the stairs, and got onto her bike.

Götz was sitting outside his workshop, beer in hand. The pavements were filling up; nearby Karl-Heine-Strasse was coming to life. Someone was playing the guitar and singing, while young people rode past on old bicycles. From time to time Götz raised his hand in greeting.

Brida didn't resist when he pulled her inside and locked the door. Nor did she resist his urgency, the silent undressing. It had to be like this.

I'm not going to be anyone's second woman, she said as she got dressed again. *I can only be number one.*

She picked up her bag, left the workshop, got on her bike, and rode off without once turning back.

✳

On the train ride up north she deleted his telephone number to avoid being tempted. Her parents collected her from the station in Neustrelitz. They then drove in the jeep along familiar roads, down flagstone tracks and sandy paths to the house by the forest that stood on its own. From the window of her old bedroom she kept looking at the lake through the trees. Sometimes it shimmered golden in the evening light, sometimes in the mornings it lay there dark and still, and then the wind would pick up, propelling waves across the water.

Her mother had time and patience. Soups were left beside Brida's bed, cups of tea were brought and taken away again, sweet things were served on small china plates, all of this until Brida was ready to talk.

The vacation passed and Brida spent it in a state of mental paralysis. She didn't work on her texts, nor did she meet up with anybody. Some days she would go walking with the dog for hours. She pushed her bike along sandy paths, went swimming in the lakes, and lay in the meadows, watching the days get shorter.

When, late one afternoon, the cranes gathered on an empty field and heralded the end of summer with their trumpet calls, as they did every year, she went hunting with her father.

The hunting season for roe, fallow, and red deer had begun on September 1. On the drive there they didn't exchange a word. Brida knew all the tracks by heart. As a child she'd refused to believe she would ever move away from here. Now she knew she would never fully come back.

Her father parked the car, fetched the rifles and binoculars from the trunk, and plodded off.

Brida had known all about hunting and slaughtering from an early age. Her father was the local chief forester. Dead animals hung in the game larder for three to four days before they were butchered and put into the deep freeze. Where the shot had been clean and the animal gutted to perfection, her father sometimes opted for a longer hanging to allow the meat to become as tender as possible. Many people couldn't bear the smell of game, but Brida always thought of it as an aroma.

Sitting together in silence in the stand, they peered through their binoculars at the surrounding fields. Both spotted the stag at the same time. Her father touched her arm, pointed at the animal, and she nodded.

As she watched the grazing stag through a hunter's telescopic sight, saw his beautiful antlers, his unsuspecting steps farther and farther away from the protection of the forest, Brida thought of Götz. Soon she would end this peaceful life. The stag stood still, she breathed calmly and pulled the trigger.

It fell at once.

A few minutes later they were kneeling beside the animal. It had not suffered. The shot had been perfect.

✳

In October, at the start of the new semester, she went back to Leipzig. Among her luggage was a cooler with frozen meat. The shop was open, as was the door to the workshop. The bell rang when Brida went in to put the meat on the counter. There was a note on the package:

Shot and jointed by Brida Lichtblau. Immediate
consumption recommended.

The bell rang a second time when she left the shop, got into the taxi that was waiting outside, and drove off.

She ignored his telephone call a few minutes later, as well as all the others that day and over the next few days.

Close to Christmas one of her tutors, Friedhelm Kröner, a successful writer himself, invited the students to his home. A jazz trio was playing in the entrance hall. The rooms were furnished sparingly but tastefully: a Biedermeier cabinet, a farmhouse table with a painted drawer, and other strikingly beautiful pieces.

Brida remembered the table well. She had been there when Götz discovered it in a barn between Prague and Brno. She was standing behind him when he placed his hands on it and said, *This one!* It was always like that— whenever the pieces felt right to the touch, when they gave away something of their history, he wanted to have them.

On the table were glasses, wine, and beer.

Everyone was relaxed. Publishing folk were on the lookout for fresh talent and Kröner made sure that those he was closest to didn't leave empty-handed. While he was commending his current favorite to an editor of a renowned literary house, Brida felt eyes on her back. Then she saw the host move away, wander past her with his arms thrown wide, and say, *Götz, my friend!*

Daniela Krien

Look at this, your table is the centerpiece of my little universe.

Soon afterward Götz came and stood beside her, took a beer, and said, *There's a writing desk in my workshop. It would be perfect for you.*

Brida took a sip of her red wine.

How's Malika? she said.

We split up three months ago.

He took a packet of cigarettes from his pocket. Smoking was permitted at Kröner's. The host came up from behind, put his arms around the two of them, and said, *Drink, smoke, and have fun!* Obeying his order, they drank and smoked and pretended they were having fun.

Nobody stopped them when they left the party together.

A full moon shone through the window.

Götz was lying on top of Brida, holding her tight, with the weight of his body, with his legs wrapped around hers, his arms on her arms, and his hands clasping her wrists. Every attempt to free herself ended with him grabbing her more firmly and pressing his body a little more heavily on her. She turned her head to one side so she could breathe and waited. Not much more happened that night, but the following morning heralded the first day of a new life.

✳ ✳ ✳

Svenja dives headfirst into the lake. She's wearing a sporty black swimsuit and a pink swimming cap. She surfaces, turns, waves, then swims away with calm, precise movements.

The children try to stand up on their floating mattress to dive in, too. They shriek and laugh, fall backward into the water, clamber back onto the bobbing island, and cry out, *Watch, Mama!,* before flopping into the lake again. Hermine wants Götz to come over to them. As each year passes she gets more attached to him. She's always been closer to her father than to Brida. Hermine had just turned two when Undine was born, deposing her sister. From then on it was Götz who settled her down at night, took her to the babysitter in the morning, and walked her to the playground after supper, where she'd go from the slide to the swings until she was tired and Götz carried her home.

Götz doesn't take much persuading. He runs into the water and it takes him only a few strokes to get to the girls. They squeal and pretend he's a shark. Brida watches them and wishes the woman doing the front crawl wouldn't come back.

The three of them larking about in the water, laughing and living completely in the moment—none of this has anything to do with her anymore. She's no longer a part of it. Götz and the girls are a family, she and the girls a different one.

When Hermine and Undine are grown up they'll probably have forgotten how Götz roared as he grabbed their thin legs and dragged them off the floating mattress, how he swam and dived with them, while Brida stood at the edge of the jetty and waved as she fought back the tears. Maybe in their memories they'll see Svenja standing there. Perhaps not a single image will remain from the time they were *one* family.

The ground beneath her moves. Children come running

down the jetty, making it tip from side to side before they dive in, too, and Brida backs away from the splashes. Far out in the lake Svenja's pink cap surfaces every few seconds. She's changed direction and is now heading back to the shore, smoothly and rapidly. When she sees Götz and the children, she'll play around with them, showing the children tricks and earning their admiration. And soon she will have Götz's child.

Brida's been out in the blazing sun for too long. Her shoulders are burning.

She wants to walk back to the manor house with Götz and the girls, look out over the lake from the terrace, and have an ice cream. Like all the other families she wants to sit with her husband and children beneath a sun umbrella, languid, heavy with heat, and absolutely certain of where she belongs.

And in the evening, when the girls go up the only real incline in the area to photograph the sunset, and to roll down the sloping meadow over and over again, she will wander along the winding path with Götz, through the uncultivated landscape, until they reach the hunting stand. In the setting sun, the raised hunters' platform will cast a lengthy shadow across the meadow. Birds will rise to catch dancing insects in the last of the light, and Götz will grasp her from behind. *Tell me what you want!* she'll whisper, and he'll tell her as clearly as he always does.

Nothing is less erotic than a man who makes no demands.

She'll give him what he wants, not only because he demands it, but because it fuels her desire too. And on the way back he'll hold her hand, not letting go until they're standing outside their cottage and Brida unlocks the door. They'll go in together, take a bottle of wine from the fridge, step out onto the terrace, and wait for the children.

Mama! Look what I can do!

Undine stands on Götz's shoulders and jumps into the water. She swims a few strokes, climbs up the ladder to the jetty, and stands in front of her, dripping wet. *Svenja can do a somersault!* she says excitedly. *Did you know that?*

Svenja's head, with its pink covering, appears by the jetty. She swiftly climbs the ladder and Götz follows. *If you don't mind*, he says, *Svenja and I are going to go on a little outing with the girls. That'll give you the afternoon to write in peace.*

Write in peace.

For years that was all she wanted.

Now that she has the children only half the time, only gets half of the children's lives, half of their joys, half of their worries, the words won't flow. Now that joint custody—the fairest way the lawyers have devised of sharing bringing up children—has given her the freedom to work undisturbed, the source has dried up.

She hates it, this arrangement that unsettles the children, that steers them from a Papa week to a Mama week and changes the apartment from Papa's into Mama's, then back again, just so everything is done equitably. Having said that, Brida wasn't prepared to relinquish custody either.

Even now, on vacation, the arrangement is adhered to fairly. The children spend half of the day with Götz and Svenja, while Brida takes over for the other half. And if, by chance, they decide to spend the day all together by the lake, they look like one big happy family.

The jetty is still in the blazing sunshine. Although there is no real danger, she feels at the mercy of the world. In a crisis she is on her own. Her face is burning, and one thought after another races through her head.

Love isn't an emotion.

Love isn't romance.

Love is an act.

Love has to be viewed from the perspective of crisis.

Everything she's written about love in the past is nonsense.

Nothing's going to change between us, Götz said after their divorce. *We'll still be close.*

But everything had changed. There was no "we" anymore.

In the past his touch and the smell of his skin had dispelled her doubts. His mere physical presence had allayed her concerns. She'd smiled and made jokes about it.

I don't need you—how often had Brida thrown these words at him? She, who prized words more than he did, had used them flippantly, underestimating their force.

Svenja is smarter. Her instincts work properly. Her girly femininity is simple, almost vulgar. She worships Götz, admiring him without any ironic filter. She is submissive, admits her weaknesses outright, even using them to boost his self-worth by saying, *You do that better than me*, and routinely leaves to him the traditional male preserves.

Either she's extremely cunning or genuinely naïve. Brida suspects it's the latter.

* * *

Her best time was when they got together again.

Brida, who now gave each year its own name, called it: *The Year of Götz.*

The trips to the east were no longer elopements. As often as she could, Brida now went with him officially, as the woman by his side.

The farther east they explored, the less sleek the world around them became; increasingly it resembled the images of her childhood in rural northern Germany. The façades of the houses were tired and dirty, the roads full of potholes, the markings faded, the trees old. The physiognomy of the people they came across stuck in her mind. The West washed traces from people's faces, the East etched them in.

They drove through time, windows down, the wind in their hair, cigarettes between their fingers and loud music playing. It was fantastic. They didn't argue, they never tired of each other, and when his hands reached for her at night, Brida hoped he would throw caution to the wind and give her a child.

The large apartment in Gohlis was a stroke of luck. The family who lived there were Götz's customers and by chance he was the first to find out about their imminent move.

Although the street was in the city center, it felt like being in a village. Few cars drove down this road because of the cobbles, gardens and undeveloped land lay between the houses, and the apartment was in a tall building surrounded by mature trees, with generous, covered wooden balconies.

When they moved in on a warm May day, the swifts returned to the city, too, and it turned out that Brida and Götz's new home was also the summer residence of some of the farthest-traveled birds.

For weeks Brida left the apartment only when it was unavoidable. The journey to the Institute was longer now, but prettier than before. It took her through a small patch of woodland, along Rosental's large meadow, across very few roads and through Johanna Park, which was in full bloom.

Living with him was easy.

He was happy when she lay down with him.

He was happy when neither of them said anything,

He was happy when they worked and ate and slept and chatted about things that had happened in their time apart.

From time to time she wished he would discuss philosophy and psychology with her and soar to higher planes until the air became thinner, leaving everything terrestrial behind. But whenever a conversation took this turn Götz would smile and beg her to stop believing he had all the answers. There were others better at that sort of thing.

At the age of twenty-one he had set out as a journeyman apprentice carpenter, and many of his views dated from this time. When a master carpenter collected him from home and accompanied him to the edge of Stuttgart, all Götz had in his bundle was a notebook and pencil. He was proscribed from working within forty miles of the city. In summer his work clothes were too warm and in winter not warm enough, and many mornings he would wake up not knowing where he would spend that night or what he would eat. Sometimes he slept outside. He traveled to Austria, Switzerland, France, Portugal, and finally Iceland, living for three years without a telephone or computer, walking thousands of miles, meeting hundreds of people, and sleeping in as many different beds.

The ten years separating Brida and Götz represented less of a gulf between them than his time as a journeyman. Götz had matured early. Scarcely anything fazed him, and he was not impressed by clever words alone. He judged people by their actions. When she asked him what he most loved about her, he said three things: her intelligent curiosity, her dedication, and her talent for creating a story from nothing. She loved him for this answer.

The rhythms of their lives were rarely in sync.

Götz liked the early mornings, Brida wrote late into the night. Often when his body clock woke him around six in the morning, he would pull her toward him and push up her nightshirt. Half asleep she would take him inside her, often lying passively on her stomach.

The sleep that followed was full of dreams. As Götz began his day in the workshop, Brida traveled through surreal landscapes, hunting animals that couldn't exist, falling from cliffs without ever hitting the ground, sleeping with men she didn't know and reaching out into the empty space beside her.

She always had breakfast alone.

Brida would often pick him up from the workshop in the evening and they would go out somewhere.

He caught the eye of women in bars, but he didn't seem to

notice as he never returned their gaze. Brida wavered between pride and anxiety. He was a handsome man, happy in his own skin, a man who followed his own moral compass, who radiated security and superiority.

When they stayed in, they watched films, read, or made love. After Götz went to bed around eleven, Brida would sit at her desk. There, with a glass of wine and in the peaceful certainty that Götz was asleep next door, she was at her happiest.

Then her characters would awaken. Once up, they moved, spoke, and acted, and all Brida had to do was to write down the moving images inside her head. When an idea came to her, the most important thing was to follow it.

Around two o'clock, or half past two at the latest, her eyes would close and she would go to sleep beside Götz in the hope that the protagonists of her stories would return the following evening. Some part of their bodies was always touching—her foot on his leg, her hand on his back, his fingertips on her hip.

She was never so productive in any other year before or since those first twelve months that they lived together. A batch of short stories, three longer pieces, and half of her first novel emerged during that time.

Black clouds are gathering above the lake in Hollershagen. A gust of wind darts beneath the ends of the towels that Svenja and Götz are lying on. Götz gets up energetically and calls the children. The first flash of lightning appears on the horizon, followed soon after by a thunderclap; the sky turns dark at a stroke and everyone whirls about. The children sort out their own things and Götz packs up everything else, but before that he places his towel around Svenja's shoulders.

Being caring—that's the difference.

And being protective.

He's only going to protect one woman. He can sleep with the two of them, but he can't look after both.

Brida walks back to the cottage barefoot and with burnt shoulders. Two hundred yards to go, one hundred and fifty, now she can glimpse the cottages between the trees. The wind is whipping up into a storm, and she is drained of all energy. Spruce needles prick the soles of her feet, and when a group of children runs past and one of them bumps into her, she staggers so badly that she has to sit down.

The weather rages around her, branches are thrown into the air. She drags herself the last few feet to the cottage, draws the curtains when she's inside, and lies down on the bed.

Love isn't the coming together of two autonomous individuals who can withdraw to their own independence at any time. The protected space of a peaceful world in which the man and woman determine on a daily basis what it means to be a man or a woman has made her forget that there is something else behind all this. An old order that has been suspended only temporarily. Should any danger approach it would immediately re-establish itself.

Brida lies next to Götz and Svenja, with only a wall separating them. She can hear them giggling.

Then the door flies open and the children are standing beside her. *We want to be with you,* they cry. *Papa and Svenja have locked themselves in, they're doing S-E-X.* They spell the letters out one by one and double up with laughter. Brida doubles up too.

Undine crawls into the bed and starts tickling her. Laughter and tears are all mixed together. She has no control over it anymore. Everything floods out.

Mama! Hermine says, horrified.

Then the child throws her arms around her.

✳ ✳ ✳

About twelve years earlier, on a cold December day, she'd been speeding through the city on her bike.

Brida had never managed the stretch between the apartment and workshop so quickly. Her hands and ears were stinging from the cold because in her excitement she'd forgotten her hat and gloves.

Götz was busy with customers. Ignoring his raised eyebrows she wandered into the workshop, took the bottle of sekt from her bag, opened it, and fetched two glasses from the small cupboard beside the sink. She cleaned the table and placed the test with the two blue stripes between the filled glasses. Then she waited.

Götz came closer, stopped, looked at the table, the test, the stripes. In his face she could see a dawning comprehension, curiosity giving way to an expression of serious surprise.

Hermine, he said. *If it's a girl, she has to be called Hermine.*

The registry office wedding took place in June. Götz's parents did little to hide their disappointment. For them, a marriage not concluded before God had no meaning. Brida's parents didn't care. The tension between the two sets of grandparents rather marred the modest celebration of close friends and relatives, but Brida felt sure that her and Götz's differences in mind-set and lifestyle were unimportant.

*

The birth was an imposition. Brida couldn't think of another way to describe it. The waves of pain that passed through her body were not subject to any control whatsoever. Forces were at work inside her. There was no way out, only this primeval energy that almost tore her apart.

And then the child.

And more waves. But this time of love, warm and soft. And with them the intimation of a different kind of pain.

Götz had fallen asleep beside her. The baby lay in a plexiglass bed, a pink plastic name band on its wrist. It was sleeping and making soft noises. Brida struggled to sit up and lifted the little bundle from its bed on wheels. She placed the baby between her and Götz and stared at it. *Hermine,* she said quietly, touching the palms of the tiny hands. The baby's fingers closed around Brida's finger, holding it tight.

Now the child was here. It had come to stay. It would need her. Every day, every hour.

The Year of Hermine was beginning.

Hermine cried.

She cried before being fed and after being fed, she cried when they went for a walk and she cried at night.

Her screams shredded all of Brida's thoughts. Whenever she crept to her desk, having laboriously gotten Hermine to sleep, she could be sure that it wouldn't be long before that shrill little voice was echoing through the apartment again, forcing her to abandon the work she'd just begun.

To begin with she was still able to manage short passages, but soon the characters fell silent and stood still.

The baby demanded her in her entirety. Every resource belonged to Hermine. If her needs were satisfied for a while, Brida felt so empty that all she wanted was some quiet and some sleep. Every day it became clearer just how much her life had changed.

Her freedom had only ever been imaginary, time restricted. Like a sweet she was permitted to taste before it was taken away from her for good. For generations of women before her, life paths had been narrower, more fixed. Suddenly Brida imagined these women must have been happier, as they would never have lived under the illusion that they could shape their own lives, never felt the disappointment when all the open doors slammed shut at once. None of the constraints on their lives were their own responsibility. The circumstances hadn't allowed for anything different.

Brida, however, had made the choices herself. She'd wanted the man and the child and instead of being content with these, she wanted to write. More than ever she wanted to write.

Götz traveled east on his own again. Although he never stayed away for longer than two or three days, and now tried to find the right pieces of furniture from estate sales closer to home, he was always out until early evening, even if the store was full and he was busy in the workshop. When he got back, Hermine was already asleep, often with Brida lying asleep beside her. Their lives were rarely in step.

About three months after the birth they made love again for the first time. It was good, nothing had changed. Late in the evening, when Hermine was asleep, Götz's sexual appetite was at its greatest. But Brida wanted him in the mornings, at the only time of day when her desire had yet to be subdued by exhaustion.

Over time, Hermine's constant crying tailed off, and after six months or so Brida began to move further afield again. Götz and she tried a few times to visit a café with the baby, but Hermine would start screaming the moment her buggy stopped. Götz's attempts to simulate movement by rocking her were fruitless. He was amused by his daughter's smartness and it didn't bother him in the slightest when they had to abandon their outing and walk back home, he with the child in his arms. Brida, on the other hand, was disappointed each time.

She resumed her studies when Hermine was nine months old and spent the mornings with a babysitter.

Götz had been against the idea. They argued like never before.

He hadn't been to daycare. His mother had stayed at home with him and his siblings until he started school. In Götz's view

these sheltered early years had been the foundation for his entire future existence. He went so far as to claim that it would
be up to Brida whether Hermine turned out happy or unhappy.

Now, East and West were more than just geographical markers.

East and West were signifiers of a right and a wrong way to
live.

Brida stayed for the first week with the babysitter as her
daughter settled in, but in the second week she would take off
Hermine's coat when they arrived and then leave her in the care
of Miriam—a tall and plump pastor's wife. When she dropped
Hermine off each morning, she told herself she was doing the
right thing. And every morning as she left the babysitter's apartment, her body told her the opposite. Hermine crawled after
her, she sat and stretched her little arms out to her. She cried
and then screamed.

Sometimes Brida would stand outside the door for a while
and listen. Until she could no longer hear her child.

In her dearly bought time she allowed herself no breaks. She
sat at her desk as if riveted there, studying for her final exams
and writing her degree novel. Some days she made good progress, on others she spent hours plucking the hair from her legs
with tweezers.

After these lapses in concentration, she felt more than ever
like a bad mother. To soothe her conscience she would pick up
Hermine after lunch, play a little with her, lie next to her during
her afternoon sleep, and then take her to see Götz in the workshop, to prove to him as often as possible that everything was
fine with their child.

Although he'd come to terms with her decision, he left her in no doubt as to what he thought of it.

Götz would blame any display of infant stroppiness, any hint of an illness or a bad night, on the fact that Brida hadn't looked after the child herself. Even on those days when everything went swimmingly, the unspoken accusation remained in the room.

His disapproval was corrosive. The harder Brida tried to do everything correctly, the more frequent were the mishaps that seemed to prove Götz right. She forgot appointments, dropped crockery, and put the washing on at too high a temperature. It was a cycling accident with Hermine in the child's seat, however, that brought on their long-overdue discussion.

That evening Götz put their daughter to bed. Hermine was lucky—she escaped unscathed, save for a few minor grazes. She sucked powerfully on her pacifier, and Götz waited until she fell silent before creeping out and quietly closing the door.

Brida was waiting for him in the kitchen. The serious discussions always took place at the kitchen table. Apart from a bruise on her thigh and minor grazing on her elbow and shoulder, nothing had happened to her, either. The red wine eased the slight pain and lent her confidence. With patience and honesty Götz and she had always found a solution, hadn't they? They were good at resolving conflict. At the end of the evening, however, they sat facing each other helplessly.

Later they stood in a silent embrace beside their daughter's bed. Hermine's breathing was calm and regular, and this peaceful sight rubbed off on the parents. Their hearts opened. Their bodies were hungry for each other.

*

Over the coming weeks Brida finished her novel. It was the last component of her course. As a substantial chunk of the story took place in an emergency room, she gave the manuscript to her GP, Dr. Gabriel. They met twice in a café, and on the first occasion the doctor invited Brida to call her by her first name. *I'm Judith*, she said modestly and smiled her perfect smile. Then she rattled off the comments she'd carefully noted in the margins in a breathless rush. Given how quickly she spoke, Brida could only guess at the speed of her thoughts. She was fascinated by Judith. For the first time in her life she felt the desire to develop a closer friendship.

At the same time she worked on the changes suggested by her editor—to her surprise she'd managed to find a publisher without any difficulty. It wasn't one of those sophisticated literary presses her fellow students published with, nor one of the larger houses with a good name. It was a publisher her professors turned their noses up at because it flooded a fiercely competitive market with books for the masses.

She'd never used her days so effectively. Although Brida barely had any sleep, she felt fantastic. After much hemming and hawing, Götz finally agreed to spend only the mornings in the workshop for a while. In the afternoons he would look after Hermine, do some of the housework and the shopping.

Like cogs in a machine they worked in tandem, everything had a purpose, and one morning the postman brought a heavy package with freshly printed books.

Brida took out one of the books and held it in her hands for a long while before opening it. Her final piece of work had not earned her a top grade. Her professors thought that while the novel was solidly crafted, it was structured too conventionally. It lacked a clearly recognizable style of its own, the signature of high artistic achievement. The content, on the other hand, revealed a profound understanding of psychological processes. In parts it read as if it had been written by someone at the end of their life rather than the beginning. But what did that matter? In her hands she had her book, her finished book. Only Hermine's birth had produced a similar feeling in her—a deep satisfaction combined with great anxiety.

She'd been allowed to have her say on the design of the cover: Playmobil figures against a white background. The way the figures were arranged reflected the relationships between the characters. LIFE PATTERNS stood in plain black lettering on the cover, and above it her name:

BRIDA LICHTBLAU

*

On the day of the launch Hermine fell ill.

She was running a high temperature and Götz canceled the babysitter for the evening. He wanted to stay with his child.

He'd accepted the situation straightaway. As usual, he hadn't expressed any regret. Normally Brida admired him for this. Whenever circumstances changed, Götz simply adapted to them without complaint. He didn't seem to harbor any resistance.

This evening wasn't any old evening, however. People Brida didn't know would be coming to hear her speak. It was the birth of a public persona; she would have to stand up and expose herself without any protection.

This evening she could have done with Götz being there.

But everything went swimmingly without him. The rows of seats in the bookshop were full, and when the whispering and murmuring stopped as Brida began to read, she felt at one with herself. The microphone accentuated the timbre of her dark, slightly rough voice, and she didn't slip up once. Afterward she signed books, answered questions, and realized to her astonishment that she liked the attention.

Her disappointment at not having Götz there had turned to relief. His quiet, supercilious manner had prevented her often enough from coming out of her shell.

Later that evening they wandered through the city: Paula Krohn, the bookseller; the editor from the publishing house; Judith; and her student friends Alma and Xandrine. They ate in an excellent restaurant and when it was time for goodbyes, Judith was the one who suggested they continue the evening.

The two of them drifted from bar to bar, flirting, letting men buy them drinks, and when Judith picked out a man she intended to take home, Brida longed for Götz to be there.

She spent the following day in a fog of nausea and exhaustion, and the day after that she discovered she was pregnant.

* * *

In Hollershagen the storm has passed. The children have run outside, the sun is warming the wet meadows, and a myriad of insects are astir in the rising steam.

Something has to happen. There are still eight days of vacation to come. Eight whole days of having to watch, smell, and listen to Svenja. Of having to put up with Svenja's small, powerful physical therapist's hands on Götz's body.

She steps onto the terrace and listens. Although it's early afternoon, she's drinking wine and smoking. Brida fancies she can feel the toxins penetrating her body, her lungs trying to expel the tar, her liver battling with the alcohol, her skin sagging, and her hair turning gray. She's gripped by a strange desire. A desire for decay and destruction.

A door opens in the next cottage. Svenja comes out onto the terrace. Her hair is wet and a fruity fragrance wafts over to Brida. Svenja stretches her body, her muscles. The expression of satisfaction on her face is testament to a good fuck.

Brida isn't ashamed at this crude thought.

The time for shame is over. As is the time for lies.

Something has to happen.

*

She barely has any memories of *The Year of Undine*.

She didn't write anything.

But there was a lot of breastfeeding, cooking, and eating.

And breastfeeding, cooking, and eating.

And sitting in playgrounds, lifting Hermine onto seesaws, helping her onto slides, all the while with Undine on her back.

She read nothing.

But there were a lot of naps, albeit always too short.

And a lot of arguments because Götz was relaxed and she wasn't. Because he was patient and she wasn't.

Undine had come at the wrong time. Her arrival was like a large, heavy paw forcing Brida's head back under a dark body of water just as she'd briefly come up for air.

* * *

Then came *The Year of Judith*.

Their friendship was like a tender love.

Before they met up, Brida would make herself look beautiful, as she'd done with Götz in the beginning, and the anticipation of seeing Judith again was similar to the excitement she'd felt with him at first.

If Judith canceled an evening, Brida was deeply disappointed.

The energy that radiated from Judith passed directly to her. After spending time with her, Brida was able to write in spite of the children. She resisted the usual distractions, was more focused and efficient, and this positive influence was why Brida kept seeking out her friend.

Judith's ability to grasp and analyze a situation, and come up with a solution within seconds, lured Brida into accepting her judgment when she was in a state of total exhaustion.

As far as Judith was concerned, the problem was Götz. He was restricting Brida, curtailing her individuality, and he was not admiring enough of her artistic achievement. He was trying to reduce her to the role of housewife, putting his own interests above hers. And although Brida felt that this wasn't true, that the truth lay elsewhere, she didn't object and described Götz as jealous, proprietorial, and small-minded. Even when Judith's eyes grew large and the expression on her face turned frosty, Brida failed to defend him, and when Judith said, *Leave this man. He's no good for you*, Brida kept quiet.

Götz smelled the danger. Although he'd met Judith only a few times and usually refrained from being judgmental about people, he didn't mince his words. She was a cold and destructive narcissist who was incapable of love, he said. But his harshness drove Brida even closer to Judith. And when he asked Brida not to see her so often, because she always came back home a changed woman, the doubts that Judith gave succor to appeared to be confirmed.

Hermine was four and Undine had just turned two when one evening Brida welcomed Götz home by telling him that she could no longer bear the restrictiveness of her life.

They hadn't seen each other in almost three days. A friend

from his journeyman years had told Götz about an estate sale not far from his hometown of Stuttgart. He went with his new, recently employed colleague to southern Germany, filled up the van, and paid a visit to Götz's parents.

Brida had bowed to necessity, even though it wasn't a good time. She had to finish a story for an anthology, Hermine was suffering from weeping conjunctivitis, and Undine was saying *No!* to everything. Judith came round the evening before his return, and Götz learned of the outcome of their alcohol-fueled conversation even before he'd taken off his shoes and hung his coat on the stand.

Götz listened without interrupting. He followed her into the kitchen, sat at the table, and let her speak, and the more Brida said, the more she felt as if Judith's words were mingling with her own, and when she started retracting some of her comments and softened her accusations, he raised his hands defensively.

Had she ever thought she was asking for too much? he asked, his voice quivering. Did she think it was possible to have everything, without any sacrifice, without any limits?

Did she seriously believe she could have children and art and culture and a husband and sex and time to read and time to do nothing and spontaneous getaways, without having to pay a price?

I am always considerate! she yelled.

There is a time for everything, Brida, he said.

Then he didn't speak for days.

✳

To begin with, Brida stayed with Judith.

She saw the children in the afternoons, took them swimming, to the playground, to the ice cream shop or the cinema, brought them back to him for supper, and returned to sleep at her friend's apartment.

The emptiness and coolness of the unfamiliar rooms was therapeutic. She slept well. Nothing imposed itself on her, nothing restricted her. No pain had to be remedied, no washing had to be done. Nobody demanded anything of her.

She spent the evenings on the sofa next to Judith. They drank wine, ate olives, cheese, and crackers, and had a look at whatever came up on the websites Judith visited frequently. When browsing horses, Judith was interested in stature, breed, age, and rideability, whereas on the dating site she checked for height, age, profession, and hobbies.

Brida thought the difference was marginal.

Sometimes she would forget the children for a brief while.

In those periods she meandered through the city, wrote a few words in cafés, took walks, visited exhibitions, browsed antique shops, and viewed apartments. But the appointments with real estate agents put an end to her levity. Questions about income and the number of children she had forced her to face the facts. She was almost through the grant that had eliminated her money worries for half a year and there wasn't another in the offing. Her current book project, meanwhile, was nothing to speak of yet.

But Götz wouldn't abandon her. If she wrote the occasional piece for the newspaper, quickly finished the book, and negotiated a decent advance, the next year or two would be sorted out.

She went to see Götz at the workshop to discuss the essentials. He had dark rings around his eyes and made no effort to be friendly. He listened to her long-winded explanations in silence. He didn't answer her, asked no questions, waited until she was finished, nodded, and saw her to the door.

Every day the children asked when she was coming home. There was never any mention of *whether*, only of *when*. Brida was evasive, talking about another place to live and an adventure and a completely different life. Hermine immediately and firmly said, *No!*

Hermine didn't want anything to be different. Then she would repeat her usual question: *When are you coming back?*

More than once Brida toyed with the idea of leaving the children behind, vanishing and starting her life from scratch. With another man in another city, and as a writer rather than a mother who wrote.

But the idea never really took shape, losing its charm whenever the girls came running toward her when she picked them up from school.

When Judith wasn't working, she was with her horse or exercising.

The insight Brida gained into Judith's day-to-day life was sobering. All of a sudden her friend's freedom seemed meaningless. Nothing in the apartment required her presence—no plant, no animal, no other person; it was merely a base, a take-off and landing pad, a storeroom. No celebrations were held here, no children played here.

The black Bechstein grand piano stood in the living room, its lid shut. She hadn't heard Judith play it once. A lilac-colored sofa dominated the rest of what was otherwise an almost empty room. The sofa was where Judith sat, ate, and worked all in one. Often, however, she would sit cross-legged on the bare parquet floor.

She spent a lot of time on her appearance. The cosmetics in the bathroom were expensive and the results spoke for themselves. Her pure, smooth skin and shining hair always made Judith look fresh. Although she was younger, Brida felt spent and worn-out by comparison. The bags under her eyes never went away.

A few times she borrowed Judith's Audi. She raced along the motorway at more than a hundred twenty miles per hour, working her way through the collection of classical music. The journey was the destination. Sometimes she would just stop off somewhere, walk for a while along a river, through a village, a forest. And with every step, the agonizing question of whether she'd chucked it all in pointlessly or whether she just needed a break hammered in her head.

After about three weeks, things became tense between them. Every day Judith came home later and sometimes not at all. It was time to go.

At the beginning of the fifth week Brida went home.

She'd already picked the children up at lunchtime.

They wandered through the weekly market, bought a watermelon, strawberries, bread, smoked char, hand-churned butter, and new potatoes. On the way home they sang songs and the girls wouldn't leave her alone for a second.

Götz didn't comment on her reappearance at first. He ate the rhubarb cake she'd bought for him, fooled around with the children, and later, when Hermine and Undine were playing in the garden, listened to Brida's explanations and apologies. When she promised never to abandon the family again, he shook his head and said, *That's enough!*

In the days that followed she kept bursting into tears. When they were all sitting at the dining table, when the children were happy and Götz touched her without thinking about it, she understood what she'd given up. Now, in retrospect, came the fear.

They made love every day and Brida couldn't get enough of his caresses. She took homemade lunches to the workshop, kept the apartment clean, tended the garden, and played and made things with the children even though she found it terribly boring.

Although Götz didn't want to hear it, she kept assuring him how sorry she was and how much she loved him.

And it was true. She did love him.

The weeks of separation seemed to Brida like a bad dream, and she named the year ahead of them after him.

✳ ✳ ✳

She's had a dreadful night. It's got nothing to do with the vacation.

Brida hasn't yet learned how to overcome her anxiety and

despair. During the daytime the thought of death proves to be helpful, but at night it merely makes her wish that death would come for her now.

Hermine and Undine sleep soundly and innocently. Because they couldn't agree on who would have which bunk, both are on top. The head of one is beside the feet of the other and vice versa. They breathe in and out in sync, in and out.

Brida tiptoes out of the room and gets back into bed. She's freezing and her heart is beating wildly.

How long can it beat like this? How long can it survive this rhythm? Her heart is going to kill her. It's going to stop. Just when she imagines she's safe.

Hers is not a good heart. It's a corrupt and stupid heart. It followed the wrong scent and was lured by the wrong voices. It will stop because it deserves to.

And the children sleep, suspecting nothing.

And Götz sleeps, suspecting nothing.

And nobody comes to take her fear away.

It's getting light. A dog barks somewhere in the forest and the last bats return from their night flight to their dark quarters behind the wooden paneling of the vacation cottage. Brida finds their silent, shadowy existence more agreeable than the bird-song that demands happiness.

She needs to talk to Götz. Have one last try.

On balance she's got more to offer than Svenja. Two children together and the best sex of his life. Didn't he tell her that it could never be as good with anyone else? That he was only able to cross boundaries with her? She'll remind him of that.

She'll remind him of the sacrifice at the beginning of their relationship and her sacrifice now. For his sake she put up with being woman number two, the secret one, and she's putting up with it again. But her rightful place is at his side.

She'll remind him of the good times and apologize for the bad ones.

She won't make any promises, having broken them too often in the past. But not making promises will show him just how serious she is. What isn't said will tell him everything. He's observant. He'll understand.

And her heart relaxes. The birdsong no longer sounds like a mockery of her suffering.

Countless toads are advancing through the damp grass in the meadow behind the house. She plants her bare feet right in the way of the cold, brown creatures, then bends to pick one up and closes her hands around it. The toad secretes a liquid. Its legs want to jump, but the hollow around it isn't big enough. Brida closes her hands even more tightly around the terrified creature.

Someone should come and wrap themselves around her, too.

She turns and looks at the windows of the neighboring vacation cottage. The roller blinds are down, the door locked.

Are they sleeping? Or are they making the child he talked about? Is he at this very moment disgorging into her open womb? Is this the moment where the path of destiny turns a corner? Or is she the one who can turn it a different way? All she has to do is ring the bell, disturb their lovemaking, interrupt what would bind those two for life.

She's desperate to rip the toad's legs off. She's so desperate to do this that she merely drops it and runs into the house.

Brida doesn't want to live without him.

She's forgotten how to be alone.

Her hands trembling, she fills the kettle and shakes some coffee powder into a cup. But then she goes outside in only her nightie, without making the coffee. She wanders the few steps to the other cottage and puts her finger on the bell.

Brida was certain she wouldn't repeat her mistake.

It had been a good year since Götz and she had gotten back together.

She seldom saw Judith now. They'd been to the Gewandhaus once and for a drink a few times, but the peculiar feeling that she had to justify herself to Judith, that she was some kind of coward, made Brida keep her distance.

Brida worked while the girls were at school, but whenever her characters started to come alive, when she could have followed them, it was time for pickup.

Like most young families, she and Götz had to make do without the help of grandparents. It was around five hours by car to Götz's parents and almost four to her own parental home. One winter vacation in southern Germany and one summer vacation in Mecklenburg plus two return visits to Leipzig each were the only times Hermine and Undine spent with their grandparents.

Brida spent the days prior to their final separation in a total haze.

Two attempts to shut herself away for a few days to write had failed. Götz had twice promised her this time-out. On both occasions, however, a job had gotten in the way, commissions that Götz couldn't turn down because they needed the income and he didn't want to lose long-standing customers.

He was the one earning the money. Since the advance for her first novel and the income from her readings, Brida hadn't contributed anything worth mentioning to the family coffers. The allowance from her parents given to her on the birth of each child had long since disappeared. Götz carried the financial burden, but he didn't complain about it.

It made Brida furious that he was so easily pleased. His composure provoked her ire. The modesty of his needs made her want more.

✳

It was in a bar that Brida met the first man who extolled those qualities of hers which Götz was critical of. Judith had made the contact, something she did effortlessly—a smile, a slight cock of the head, tossing back her hair and jiggling her feet in those high heels. Only Brida saw the scorn in her eyes because, yet again, it had been too easy. Judith focused on the man's friend, leaving him to Brida.

This man, whose name she no longer recalls, had been impressed. A husband and children and writing—how did she cope? He wrote himself, but couldn't imagine doing anything else besides. Not only did he appear to understand the impatience and anger that sometimes brewed inside her, he defined it as the sign of an energetic artistic personality. She never saw him again, but she often thought about their conversation.

The second man was M.

In fact she wasn't supposed to be at the school summer party. She'd intended to write in a place far away from Götz and the children, but once again something had gotten in the way.

She'd often bumped into M., mostly at afternoon pickup. And now he sat beside her at the edge of the sandpit, tapping away at his phone.

His son stood hesitantly, legs apart, in front of the sandcastle Undine had built. Spade in hand and chewing his lower lip, he seemed to be mulling over some serious question. Then, out of the blue, he jumped and landed right on top of the sandcastle.

Instead of being angry, Undine looked at him quizzically. With a sigh she left the sandpit and went to sit on a swing. From there she watched what happened next.

At that moment she resembled Götz so closely that Brida couldn't take her eyes off her. Her superiority was most apparent in the expression on her face. The boy's pleasure in destroying her efforts provoked in her curiosity and pity, but nothing more. She didn't need to strike back. Her strength was the ability to immediately accept the situation for what it was and to move on to a different game. Brida felt anger fermenting inside. It wasn't the boy who made her cross, but her own child.

M. apologized. *What's gotten into you, Linus?* he bellowed at his son, gripping both his arms.

I've no idea why he did that, he said when Linus wrested himself free and ran away.

In the sandpit their bare feet were almost touching. He was wearing blue linen trousers and an airy white shirt. He'd taken off his fine leather flip-flops.

It was one of those summer days that Brida liked best—no wind, and so hot that wearing clothes was merely a matter of decency, not necessity.

He looked at her in a direct way, but without being suggestive.

I know how I can make up for it, he said, taking a card out of his wallet and handing it to her. *Next week we're opening a new exhibition. Why don't you come along and have a glass of wine.*

Maybe, she said. He smiled and nodded.

The strikingly ordinary woman who now sat down beside him in the sandpit wore the same wedding ring as his—plain, matte, white gold. *I'm so glad to meet you*, she said to Brida. *I read your novel and really loved it.*

She saw no hint of embarrassment in his eyes, no flinching. She understood what those eyes were saying.

In the days that followed, doubts began to gnaw at her. Was M. just being friendly? Did he smile at everyone like that?

On the evening of the vernissage it was easy enough to slip out of the apartment. Götz was happy to spend time with the children, and to be able to go to bed early. He was exhausted after the twelve-hour days he'd been putting in recently.

When Brida entered the gallery, she was sure there had been

a misunderstanding at the school party. There stood M., surrounded by people. He looked fantastic, with his arm around a young woman, who Brida later found out was the artist whose pictures hung on the walls. As Brida looked at the large photographs she felt stupid. She neither understood the message behind the images, which all featured the same table, nor could she work out what had brought her here.

Slowly, and as discreetly as possible, she moved toward the exit, jostling past the people streaming in. Outside, she lit a cigarette and leaned wearily against the wall of the old factory building. She closed her eyes momentarily. When she opened them again M. was standing in front of her. Very close, his hands in his trouser pockets and visibly delighted.

Their first sex in a hotel room was intense. It was a Monday and M. had the day off as the gallery was closed.

They'd taken the lift upstairs in silence, let themselves into the room, gotten undressed, and thrown themselves at each other.

She couldn't look at him; it was too intimate. He turned her head toward him almost violently. She cried and wriggled from his grasp.

Do you regret this? he asked. *No*, she replied, *it's not that*. She pushed her back against his tummy, took his arm, and placed it around her.

She told him too how hard it was to write with children around, and that bringing up her girls wasn't enough for her— her purpose in life was a different one. He laughed bitterly. How he wished, he said, that his wife harbored even a trace of this desire. Ever since their son had been born, he told Brida, nothing else mattered to her apart from the child.

Brida snuggled up to him even more. What he'd just said sounded like the invitation to a better life.

She was fertile ground for his words on that first afternoon and on all those that followed. Her conscience remained curiously clean.

You and I, M. said, *we're free individuals. We stay if people leave us alone, we go if people try to possess us.*

As he compared them to plants in dry soil and animals behind bars, he held her hand and looked at the ring on her finger. *Art and a bourgeois marriage don't mix well*, he said. Brida ought to live and broaden her experience. How could she describe vividly what she didn't see or feel?

Then they realized how wonderfully well they understood each other, and how good they felt together. Each time they met it felt ever more familiar and it got harder to say good-bye.

Brida only ever hooked up with M. during the daytime, when the children were at school and Götz in his workshop. By the time he came home in the evening, Brida had eliminated all traces of her lover. Her plaited hair would be wound around her head again like a crown, her hands busy chopping vegetables and her mind apparently on the children.

Götz failed to notice a thing. He was friendly and caring; she found this impeccable behavior of his unbearable. Down below the children played on the small patch of lawn between the rosebushes, which Brida had planted in her first summer here. Hermine unraveled the garden hose and drenched Undine, who had been sitting naked in the grass, picking daisies. The two of them squealed with delight.

Before they could look up at her, Brida stepped back into the kitchen. All the doors and windows to the apartment were open as Götz was trying to get a draft going through, but the air was totally still. Fruit flies circled the sliced watermelon on the table, several summer chafers had strayed inside and droned as they knocked into cupboards and windowpanes. She could hear Götz showering in the bathroom and realized that happiness was throwing itself at her in abundance at that very moment.

The following morning Götz took the children to school. Brida left the breakfast things on the kitchen table, ignored the mountain of washing in the bathroom, and sat on the balcony with her laptop and a pot of coffee. She smoked a cigarette, resolved never to see M. again, and opened a new document.

She chose the title *Hunter and Hunted* and began to write.

The first sentence gave way to a second, and the output continued to flow until the telephone rang. Undine had been sick, while Hermine was pale and complaining of a tummy ache, the director of the school said. The children had to be picked up at once and would not be allowed back until they had certification from a doctor that they were better. It was probably a rotavirus infection, the director assumed.

It was just after 10 a.m. They had Götz's telephone number on file in the school too. If everything had gone according to plan, Brida could have worked for another four and a half hours. That day and on the two that followed she barely took in what was happening around her. Like a sleepwalker she looked after the children and washed their beds and nighties every time they were sick before they made it to the toilet. The characters from her embryonic novel accompanied her, and the children were too sick and weak to be surprised that their mother was talking to invisible people.

Hermine and Undine felt better by the fourth day, the weekend, and now Brida had the virus as well. She vomited for two days, with diarrhea and a temperature, and dragged herself from the bedroom to the bathroom and back again. Götz brought her tea and disinfected everything she had touched. And he even escaped the virus.

She spent the Monday in bed, too, and on Tuesday, when she'd drawn her chair up to the desk, opened her laptop, and, as always, cast a glance at the framed portrait of Carson McCullers, she placed her fingers on the keyboard and waited.

Nothing happened.

She stared at the screen and read the pages she'd already written.

Nothing.

Brida sweated, trembled, and was struck by the eerie feeling that she was no longer herself. The familiar surroundings of her balcony, the apartment, and the garden now seemed alien, and as she sat there in this altered state of perception, M. sent her an obscene text message.

She laughed, then she cried, then her thoughts confused her before becoming chaotic. It felt as if her skull were bursting. She wanted to scream, but the only noise she emitted was a wail that had nothing to do with her voice. Now she was shaking so badly that she gripped onto the edge of the desk with both hands and thought, *I'm having a nervous breakdown.*

In hindsight she couldn't have said how long she'd spent crying and shaking, because her sense of time went awry too. She lay in bed until the afternoon, the curtains drawn, and when pickup time approached, she called Götz and told him he had to collect the children.

Brida didn't get up again until suppertime. She sat at the table with Götz and the children but was unable to eat a mouthful.

Straight after supper Götz took the children to bed, put on an audiobook for them, and came back to the kitchen where Brida was still sitting. Götz filled two glasses with white wine, added a couple of ice cubes to each, arranged the chairs on the balcony, and put out an ashtray for Brida.

Then he listened to her talk, nodding occasionally and mumbling *I understand* more than once. But when Brida screamed, *For Christ's sake, how could you understand?*, he left it at that.

It ought to have been clear to her that there were only two possible ways out of this conversation. The logical consequence of one was the end of their relationship, and she was certain Götz wouldn't let that happen.

He spoke in his usual calm way. His superiority was not an intellectual one—in this area she beat him hands down. Rather, it was based on emotional stability. He found it easy to act in a way that worked for him. He knew his limits and didn't overstep them.

Of course he didn't want her to be unhappy, he said, and he was fully aware that the children couldn't be the only raison d'être in Brida's life; she wasn't that sort of woman. And she heard the disappointment in each of his words.

But? she asked.

Götz clasped his hands and rested them on the table between them. He avoided her gaze, but his voice was firm. *How do you imagine it could work? I can't look after the children half the time. That would be impossible.*

His jaw became angular and the muscles twitched.

The workshop and the shop are our livelihood. You have to face up to the fact that you're going to have to give up writing for a while. And if you can't accept that, then we'll have to separate.

✳

Had another way been possible?

She often asked herself this question later.

In further fruitless conversations she brought up the subject again, and a new side to Götz emerged. He spoke with bitterness about having split up with Malika for her sake. Because he'd been able to think only of Brida. Because she'd given him that fucking meat. Because at a time when he'd just started to forget her, she'd burst back into his life with that fucking meat. And yet Malika was precisely the sort of woman who'd wanted everything that Brida rejected.

✳

The solution they agreed upon was the bird-nesting arrangement.

In their moment of agreement something strange happened. The pride they felt at having acted like sensible grown-ups in order to arrive at such a compromise led them to open a bottle of champagne and sleep with each other.

The sex was more intense than ever, taking them to a new level.

Everything seemed possible again.

Brida met M. only once more. She didn't need him any longer.

It was easy to come up with a name for that year. She named it after herself.

*

Her finger is on the bell. Her reflection stares at her from the glazed door. A madwoman in a nightie. Whatever she says dressed like this, Götz won't be able to take it seriously.

She turns and goes back.

The children have woken up and a Rihanna song is coming from their room. *Like diamonds in the sky,* Hermine sings theatrically, but when Undine joins in, Hermine snaps harshly at her and for a moment the squeaky voice falls silent. Brida opens the door. *Good morning, sweeties,* she says. Then she turns to Undine and says, *Of course you can sing too.*

Her second-born behaves as if she's trying to make up for her accidental existence by being unassuming, while the planned child, Hermine, imposes her demands on life. Brida finds it easier being a mother to Hermine. Hermine doesn't give her a bad conscience, because she is just as volatile as Brida and can be just as angry, too. *Do you want breakfast?* she calls out to them. *Later*, Hermine calls back.

Brida takes a fresh towel from the cupboard, ties her hair in a bun, gets into her swimming suit, and puts on a dress.

I'll be back in twenty minutes, she says loudly.

She walks barefoot to the lake across the cool, dewy meadow, hoping she'll be the only one swimming this morning.

The leaves of the water lilies lie on the surface like small green islands. The lake is darkly silent.

She walks to the end of the jetty, puts her things on the wooden bench, and slowly climbs down the steps. With every inch she descends into the cold water she feels more animated, and when she submerges herself fully and takes her first strokes, she feels stronger and better than she has in ages. Each time she surfaces it's like finding hope, each gasp of air like breathing pure life. She'd completely forgotten what this was like.

Brida swims fast and without looking around until she gets halfway across the lake. Then she flips onto her back and stares up at the sky. The sun hasn't yet risen above the tops of the trees. Two swans drift past; Brida freezes.

She swims back with powerful strokes.

When she climbs the ladder to the jetty, she's shivering so much that her teeth chatter. She peels off her bathing suit and dries herself with rapid, rough movements until her skin is red and warm. Then the jetty shakes with someone else's footsteps. She stands perfectly still, the towel wrapped tightly around her body.

He places his arms around her. His hands reach for the towel and pull it away. *We've got to stop doing this,* Götz says, *but I don't know how.*

Götz dives headfirst into the lake and swims to the other side. Brida watches him from the bench. She doesn't want to wash anything of him off her. She gets up, gathers her things, and heads back to the cottage. Now she's looking forward to breakfast. Götz, she, and the children will sit at the table without Svenja. They'll be a family.

Svenja got an attack of cystitis in the night and sat on the toilet in pain and with a temperature until the morning. She's in the nearest town waiting to be seen by a doctor.

Brida is convinced that she's responsible for Svenja's illness. When Götz was still together with Malika and slept with her one day and with Brida the next, she suffered in exactly the same way.

Götz sits beside her with a steaming cup of coffee. When she catches his guilty look, Brida knows that these few hours without Svenja are only the illusion of a possibility.

Once upon a time she believed that her life consisted of possibilities and she simply had to choose. But when the children arrived, certain patterns emerged. Rules needed to be observed. No judge would punish noncompliance; life itself did that.

She looks at the children, then at Götz. He's made his decision—she can see it.

Hermine chats chirpily about the photography course she'd like to attend, and the bat walk in the evening. Undine thoughtfully chews her roll with jam.

Götz doesn't appear to be hungry. From time to time he glances at his mobile.

Through the large window Brida looks up at the shining blue sky.

The perfect day is beginning.

✳

It's not yet midday, but she's already packed her luggage into the car and returned the keys to reception. She goes to the lake with the children one last time. Undine takes her hand and holds it very tight. Hermine goes on ahead. Brida gave the children the choice and both said they wanted to stay.

She swims out with them again, marvels at Hermine's diving skills, and praises Undine's cautious jumps from the jetty.

Brida keeps the good-byes short. She kisses and hugs the children, turns to Götz and Svenja, raises her hand with a smile, and drives off.

They're visible in the rearview mirror, standing like a family at the gate to the vacation resort, waving wildly. Brida hoots, puts her foot down, and can hardly make out the road through the veil of tears. She drives into this summer's day as if through thick fog.

✳

Early that evening she parks the car outside the house, leaves the heavy bags in the trunk, empties her overflowing mailbox, and climbs the steps to her apartment.

She's met by silence and the smell of warm, stale air. Opening the door to the balcony, she goes out, glances at the withered flowers in the wooden planters, then scours the sky for swifts. It's the beginning of August. She's too late; they've already flown.

Brida makes coffee, fetches the long-life milk from the store cupboard, and gathers up the full moth traps. *Animal cemeteries*, Hermine calls them. It occurs to her that she hasn't named any years recently. *The Year of Brida* was the last, and much time has passed since.

She closes the doors to the children's rooms to avoid having to look at the mess, goes to her desk, starts up her laptop, and opens a new document.

The story she's going to tell has a happy beginning and a happy ending.

One Summer, she writes, then adds on the line below, *by Brida Lichtblau*.

PART FOUR

Malika

Malika tightens the bow.

She runs the bow hairs across the rosin, places the violin in position, and warms up with a few scales. Her feet are bare and hip-width apart. The long, colorful, flowery dress swings to the rhythm of her movements.

For days her sister's suggestion has been rattling around her head. A suggestion that only Jorinde could make. As if everything were possible. As if there were no boundaries. As if a person were a blank piece of paper that anything could be written on.

She'd declined. Of course. And yet the idea won't stop nagging at her.

The bank of clouds has passed, and sunlight falls onto the tear-shaped glass crystal by the window. Felicitas is lying between two flowerpots. She stands up and stretches, then swipes the crystal with her paw. Rainbow-colored dots begin to dance on the bookshelf opposite.

Malika puts down the violin, loosens the bow screw, and returns the instrument to its case. There's no point in practicing today.

She runs her finger along the spines of the books. The spectral colors on her hand quiver in time to the swinging crystal.

She stops when she gets to a slim volume, takes the book from the shelf, and opens it. Yellow Post-its are stuck to many of the pages. Malika knows entire passages by heart.

Recently, when she heard about the novella's publication, she cycled that same day to the bookshop in the city center. She took the escalator to the first floor and saw the red locks of the bookseller emerge from behind a table of books. Her pregnancy was evident, which made Malika feel a twinge.

As soon as she caught sight of Malika she raised a hand in greeting and said without prompting, *That's good timing! We've got a new book by your favorite author.* With her bulging belly she waddled to the table with the new releases, picked up a volume with a dark-blue jacket, and held it out to Malika. *It's a big love story,* she said.

Shortly afterward Malika left the shop with a signed copy of *One Summer.* Before she got on her bike she ran her index finger over the name written in blue ink.

Brida Lichtblau.

She doesn't know how many times she's read *One Summer* now.

In Brida Lichtblau's first three books the male characters occasionally had some of Götz's features, but they were still very different from the man Malika was looking for in each line. This book alone got him just right.

She opens *One Summer* at random.

> Oda cried in her sleep again. She suppressed her
> sobbing as best she could to avoid being heard through
> the thin wall that separated her from Hans and Lydia.

Malika smiles. She hopes that fiction overlaps with reality here, that Brida is Oda and that she suffered just as Malika did.

It still hurts, even after so many years.

Felicitas senses everything. She jumps down from the windowsill, lopes over, and presses herself against Malika's legs. Her tail stands straight upright and her purring demands a stroke.

Crouching down, Malika ruffles the cat's fur.

It's an hour or so before she needs to be at the music school, where she'll have to listen to a sweet but untalented nine-year-old with ambitious parents play open strings with anything but clean bowing. Sometimes the girl cries, in which case Malika gets out a packet of sweets and plays something for her.

The girl is followed by a seven-year-old, gifted, but with an attention span of five minutes max. Malika is always having to refocus him with new tricks and games.

The reward for her patience goes by the name of Lola, her pupil with the greatest potential. Twelve years old, short, and unusually diligent. Her mouth is usually contorted into a dogged grimace and she rarely smiles. But when she plays, her face relaxes.

That evening Malika is off to her parents' to celebrate. For as long as she can remember there's been music at home for her mother's birthday. Her father calls on his colleagues and throws together a string quartet. Today they're going to play a Brahms piano quintet.

She and her sister will perform too. Jorinde is going to sing an Else Lasker-Schüler poem set to music, accompanied by Malika on violin, and their father will play the piano part himself.

*

Before reunification, their parents' apartment was a meeting point, a cultural hub with Helmut and Viktoria at its center. Friends called the couple Beauty and the Beast, and there were times in Malika's life when she was absolutely certain she couldn't be the child of these dazzling parents.

Her mother's delicate figure was in stark contrast to her father—a panting walrus with an infectious laugh. He played cello in the orchestra, but his piano playing was well above average too. Viktoria had also dreamed of becoming a musician, but her voice wasn't good enough to make the grade as a classical singer; her tiny hands could barely span an octave, which ruled out studying the piano as well.

Instead she became a musicologist, reviewing new classical releases for a radio station and teaching at the university.

There was a constant flow of people in and out of their apartment: musicians, artists, writers, people from television and radio, doctors and university professors. Malika and Jorinde were present, too, though nobody actually looked after them. Jorinde would move nonchalantly among the crowds of grownups, dancing, singing, and taking sips from glasses that were left scattered around. Everybody liked her, everybody laughed at her antics. She skillfully imitated the mannerisms of individual guests, and no one doubted that one day the stage would be her home.

By contrast, Malika sought out quiet corners and leafed undisturbed through the large illustrated books that normally were only brought out under Mother's supervision for fear of children's greasy fingers. She liked the Renaissance and Baroque painters best of all.

On some of those evenings the parents forgot to put their children to bed, and so they would fall asleep wherever they happened to be sitting and wake up the next day, fully clothed, in a smoky room. Nobody ever asked the children what they thought of this.

When the wall came down, these social events became rarer. And for a while after the currency union they didn't take place at all.

Restructuring of all aspects of life took time, priorities changed.

Helmut seemed to calmly accept the Noth family's loss of importance, whereas Viktoria visibly suffered.

Jorinde missed the noisy life, too, she missed all the attention and admiration from her parents' friends. The only one who enjoyed the unusual peace was Malika.

*

Now the sun is pouring into the room.

Malika lets down the roller blinds on all the south-facing windows. Summer is only a pleasure for slim people.

She takes a cold shower, then wanders naked through the apartment and opens the wardrobe in her bedroom. Most of her clothes are long and loose-fitting, and the few pairs of trousers have an elasticated waist. Malika plumps for a black silk dress with large rose blooms, takes fresh underwear from a drawer, and a long pearl necklace from her jewelry case.

What she likes about summer is the flight from the city. The streets, shops, and museums are pleasantly empty. Sometimes you can't see a single car on a road that is usually heavy with traffic, and occasionally Malika will just stand there and stare.

She already knows she's going to be ill tomorrow. The evening will sap all her energy. Her body will produce its customary attack of migraine with scintillating scotoma and vomiting.

If Jorinde weren't coming, she might escape the psychosomatics. But her sister is going to be there. She'll bring her children and want to talk about the proposal. And Ada and Jonne will stand there in front of Malika like promises.

She gathers together the music for her pupils, packs a bottle of water and a roll-on deodorant, and fetches her violin. As she's going down the stairs the telephone rings in her apartment. She pauses, then shakes her head and carries on. On the second-floor landing her mobile rings. Without looking she feels for the phone in her bag. It's Viktoria, asking her to come earlier and help with the canapés.

*

When her parents decided they wanted their children to call them Helmut and Viktoria, Malika was sixteen and Jorinde fourteen. As expected, Jorinde didn't have a problem not saying Mama and Papa anymore, but Malika was reluctant to become quasi-friends with her parents.

She still refuses to abbreviate Viktoria to Vicky.

Malika is dreading the moment when Jorinde and Torben breeze in that evening with their children and say *Vicky!*, their arms open wide. Sometimes, when she's alone in her apartment, she says Vicky-Ficky-Fucky out loud, over and over again.

At some point when she was a teenager Malika realized why Viktoria went out almost every evening when Helmut was touring with the orchestra. She often didn't come back until late at night, or even the following morning. The notion that her mother had sexual needs disgusted Malika. But she found it even worse that it wasn't only her father who should satisfy them.

It all came to a head one cold November evening after the border had been opened.

Her parents were celebrating. Helmut had painted the words JOYFUL, COOPERATIVE ACTION on a cloth banner that hung above the big double doors to the sitting room.

The atmosphere was highly charged. Viktoria had started drinking that morning and by dinner there wasn't a single guest who was still sober.

Rüdiger was one of the last to turn up. They called him Roofing-Felt-Rudi—in the GDR he'd managed to get hold of roofing felt for some of his friends' houses, despite the constant shortages. Malika liked him. She felt flattered to be talked to by a philosopher and poet. He treated her like an adult even though she'd just turned sixteen.

When he arrived, everyone was gathered in the kitchen, around twenty people in all. He waded straight into the conversation; at that moment they were talking about those people who'd once supported the building of the wall. He mentioned the playwright Peter Hacks straight away, desperately trying to remember a certain quotation.

Helmut, where do you keep your Hacks? he called out, and Malika's father replied, *In the library next to the ax!*

The Hacks next to the ax! Rudi laughed like crazy. Viktoria joined in and flung her head against his arm as if she would fall over unless he supported her. And Rudi went to fetch the volumes of Hacks from the room in the apartment where the chopping block stood, where every wall was lined with firewood or bookshelves.

Then they talked about what would happen now.

About the end of the GDR. The end of a great idea. The end in general and about the beginning, too, and freedom.

Malika watched her father try several times to say something, but he couldn't get a word in. She was carried away by waves of pity. He wasn't as euphoric as the others and only half as drunk. Viktoria's best friend, Ruth, kept interrupting him. She rolled her eyes, imitated him, and laughed in his face. The mood became more and more edgy. Some agreed with her father, who stoically repeated his belief that the country should go its own, third way, to avoid being swallowed up. This small group broke away and relocated to the music room. Malika joined them.

When they came back, Rüdiger and Viktoria had vanished. Helmut looked around. He went from the kitchen into the hallway and stood there for a while. Suddenly he jerked into motion. Malika followed him unnoticed.

He opened the door to the wood-chopping room and peered in.

Rüdiger stood behind Viktoria, his trousers around his ankles. Her skirt was up over her back and, legs apart, she was bent over the chopping block, panting. Her knickers lay on the scratched parquet floor.

Helmut quietly closed the door, turned, and gave a start when he saw Malika standing there. And she had seen what he had seen.

In the days that followed she waited in vain for an explanation. Before every encounter with her father she wavered between fear and expectation. She sought his gaze, but he avoided looking her in the eye, was sullen, silent, and rarely at home.

Viktoria seemed unable to make any connection between Helmut's bad mood and what had happened with Rüdiger. She laughed and called him *Grumpy*, or *Sourpuss*.

For the first and only time Malika took Jorinde into her confidence. In a roundabout way she told her sister about the upsetting sight, but when Jorinde finally understood, she just pulled a face and said, *You're a pervert. Vicky would never do anything like that.*

Malika decided to do everything differently from her parents. In bed at night she envisioned her future family. It wouldn't be spectacular, but loving and intact. Each child would be loved the same, none preferred, none sneered at.

How many times she pictured holding and breastfeeding her own baby. The further her imagination drifted into the future, the more children she was surrounded by. At the point where the corresponding husband appeared, Malika would usually fall asleep.

*

She closes the door to her teaching room and puts the heavy bunch of keys into her bag. Lola was a delight, as ever. She doesn't even complain when she's given dreary exercises to practice. Malika extended the lesson by twenty minutes today because the girl wanted to play one of her own compositions. Now Malika hurries to the exit and sets off for her parents'.

If you look at it on a map, most of her life is played out in an acute triangle. The greatest distance is between her parents' home and the music school, the shortest between her own apartment and her parents'.

There was a time when there had been a healthier distance between Malika and her parents, when she, too, was with a man and seemed to be on the verge of starting her own family. But now that there's no lover making a claim on her time anymore, Helmut and Viktoria do it as often as they like.

*

One day Jorinde moved away, as expected.

It might as well have been New York instead of Berlin—the difference would only have been in the mind.

When their mother was diagnosed with breast cancer, Jorinde was filming in France. Malika was with Viktoria through all the difficult times. When their father had his defective aortic valve removed and a new one made of animal tissue implanted, Jorinde's son, Jonne, had just been born. It was Malika who visited her father every day and soothed her mother's worries. When their parents' apartment was broken into, Jorinde stayed in Berlin for the International Film Festival. Helmut and Viktoria were incredibly understanding.

Nothing had changed.

Jorinde had always been their darling, their pride and joy.

All those years ago, when they came out of school together, it was Jorinde who babbled away indiscriminately the moment they left the classroom. Usually it was about something she absolutely had to have. *I've always wanted one of those*, she would say, flinging her arms around their mother's neck—singing, chatting, and fluttering her eyelashes—and although nobody had heard her articulate that particular wish before, it was fulfilled on the grounds that she'd wanted it for *so long*.

Malika only spoke when her mother's attention had long been exhausted.

When they were teenagers, too, that awful time of physical and emotional upheaval, it was chiefly Jorinde who kept their parents on their toes. She wasn't interested in negotiation, nor in any prohibitive rules. She smoked, drank, and got a tattoo without telling them. With her radical left-wing friends she scrawled and sprayed popular slogans on refurbished buildings. Jorinde was responsible for many a SMACK A COP or GERMANY DIE.

But the event that particularly stands out in their parents' memory relates to Malika.

On the morning of the Young Musicians regional competition, Malika smashed her bow. She was seventeen. The solo assessments for string instruments at the Johann Sebastian Bach music school started at 10 a.m. First place would have gotten her into the national competition, and Malika had a fairly decent chance.

Viktoria woke Malika at half past five so she could have breakfast in peace and then practice for an hour or two. At six o'clock she came into the bedroom again and at 6:30 she pulled off her daughter's duvet. When Malika was still at the breakfast table at eight o'clock, Viktoria took the violin from its case, tightened the bow, and began tuning the instrument.

I'm not practicing anymore, Malika said. *I've practiced enough.*

These words were followed by the menacing silence that Malika knew only too well. She cowered and ate her chocolate muesli, her eyes fixed on the table.

How stupid can you be? Viktoria exploded. *This is your one chance! Most people would be delighted to get an opportunity like this once in their life, and they'd prepare properly rather than stuffing themselves with muesli and getting fat. You could become a star, Malika! A star!*

She held out the violin and bow to Malika, who stood up, took the bow, and whacked it as hard as she could against the edge of the table.

She even surprised herself. Holding the broken bow she stood there without moving a muscle. Her mother's expression had frozen. In their bewilderment, her pretty, slightly asymmetrical features looked grotesque, but instead of another tirade of abuse she calmly came up with a plan.

They had to find another bow. The audition was all that mattered.

At that moment Malika saw a way out. If she won the competition, everything would only get worse.

While Viktoria was on the phone Malika went back into her room, closed the door, and turned the key. She put on the rock and post-punk mixtape that her parents loathed and fell onto her bed. PiL's "This Is Not a Love Song" boomed from the loudspeakers, drowning out Viktoria's screaming, which had just begun on the other side of the door accompanied by a furious rattling of the handle.

This day entered the Noth family history as *the day when Malika destroyed her life*.

It was Jorinde who fulfilled Viktoria's dreams. When she graduated from the Ernst Busch drama school, all the sleepless nights and worries she'd been responsible for were forgotten.

∗ ∗ ∗

Malika took a year's break after her violin studies, and at the end of the teacher training course that followed she went straight to her parents' with her certificate. She'd scored top marks in almost every subject.

On the way she remembered that Helmut was touring with the orchestra in Asia. For a moment she contemplated postponing the visit. Since Viktoria had hit menopause her mood swings had been more pronounced than usual. Without Helmut to keep things on an even keel there was a greater likelihood of them having a row. But surely even her mother would be thrilled at Malika's grades.

She quickened her pace, gave the bell three short rings, took the stairs rather than the lift, and pushed past her mother into the apartment. Instead of greeting her, Viktoria looked at Malika quizzically. She had no makeup on and a towel was wrapped around her head.

Is this a bad time? Malika asked.

No, no, Viktoria muttered, closing the door.

Malika threw down her bag, took out the certificate, and held it out to her mother. *Yes, just a minute.* Viktoria wandered down the hall to the bathroom and appeared soon afterward with her hair combed and a calmer expression on her face. *So, show me,* she said.

She took the certificate and searched frenetically for her reading glasses, which were hanging from a cord around her neck. Once she'd put them on and adjusted them several times, she smoothed a slight crease in the upper right-hand corner of the paper with exaggerated care. Only then did she seem to realize what it was. Her eyes moved slowly from top to bottom and from left to right. She nodded, then said, *Music teacher . . . when I think what you could have become.*

The migraine that came on as soon as Malika got home was worse than usual. The extreme restriction of her field of vision forced her to crawl to the bathroom. She threw up three times, then made it to the bedroom, where she heaved herself into bed and lay there motionless.

She wished that a powerful emotion such as hatred could have armed her with the right words. But when she'd stood facing her mother, all she'd felt was a deep, crippling disappointment.

*

Over the next few weeks Malika left the apartment only to shop. Her mother's first telephone call began with the words *Oh don't be so sensitive!* and ended with a halfhearted apology. Malika ignored the rest.

She watched every season of *E.R.*, ate whatever she fancied, stopped washing her hair, and left her violin in its case. When she met an acquaintance in the supermarket who peered with curiosity at her belly, Malika preempted her and said, *I'm not pregnant, I'm just fat.*

Gradually she fell into a visible state of neglect. Bouts of howling alternated with food binges, and sometimes she would crawl into a corner of her apartment and imagine that her body wouldn't be found until the neighbors complained about the smell. She was tired but she barely slept, and eventually this led to a doctor's visit. The over-the-counter medicines weren't having any effect and Malika hoped to get a prescription for something stronger.

To her disappointment, Dr. Judith Gabriel's office didn't have a single gossip mag. *Cicero* was being read by an elderly lady, and Malika wasn't in the mood for *Rondo Magazine for Classical Music and Jazz*.

Soft piano came from two speakers—Bach's *French Suites*. The walls were covered with pictures of a haughty-looking horse. A photograph of the nag was even flaunted above the reception area. Its coat shone a golden brown in the evening light, and at other times it looked almost black.

Malika's antipathy toward Dr. Gabriel grew. She didn't like horses or horsey people.

Her whole family had been transferred to the young female doctor when old Dr. Uhlenbrock retired. Malika had considered switching GPs several times. The look on Judith Gabriel's face held the usual scorn she expected from disciplined, sporty people. They regarded being overweight as a manifestation of weakness and immoderation, or at best it was down to an illness. During one visit Frau Gabriel recommended Malika join a newly opened gym.

But the conspicuously tight organization of the practice kept waiting times short, and Dr. Gabriel seemed to be a competent doctor.

A man entered the office with a towel wrapped around his left hand. The blood was seeping out and running down his arm. He waited patiently for the receptionist to finish her call, then explained that he was a carpenter and had slipped with a wood saw. He asked if he could sit down in the waiting room. When the receptionist noticed the blood, she hurried to see her boss.

He'd been sitting beside Malika for barely a couple of minutes when Dr. Gabriel called him in. He got up, smiled, shrugged apologetically, and disappeared into the consulting room.

It was as if Malika had been stunned. Her eyes were fixed on the spot where he'd been sitting. In the upholstery of the bench there was a slight indent and his smell still hung in the air.

Then the door flew open again and the assertive voice of Judith Gabriel called out, *Siegrun!* The receptionist dropped everything and ran in.

How Malika would have loved to join her.

The frisson his physical proximity had triggered in her was strong. The tingling in her tummy was so intense that she pressed both her hands against it. She imagined being his wife, pictured Dr. Gabriel talking to both of them and giving Malika instructions for looking after his injured hand.

Then he came out of the consulting room. Without glancing at her he took a prescription from reception, said good-bye, and left the office.

Y

One week later he was in front of her in the queue at the cinema. Malika had used the waiting time to let her pupils know that there would be no violin lessons in the coming fortnight. She'd been asked to replace a violinist in a large orchestra, an offer her father might have had a hand in.

In her measured way she typed a wordy explanation into her smartphone and noticed a faint odor.

It was him. She could tell, even without looking up.

He was standing right in front of her, and like Malika he was on his own.

Malika did a countdown of every person in front of them. Just before it was his turn she decided she'd follow him into whichever film he went for.

When he was at the counter, her mind was fleetingly paralyzed by disappointment. He bought a gift token for two tickets. From his trouser pocket he took a crumpled leather wallet and paid.

She wouldn't bump into him by chance again.

How's the hand? she asked hastily as he turned away. He stopped, taken aback. *You sat beside me in the doctor's office.*

And so began what ought to have begun differently, for nothing was further from Malika's mind than to play the conqueror.

✳

She found it easy to eat less and take more exercise. Colleagues paid her compliments and for the first time she took seriously the positive feedback she got from her pupils and their parents. She saw herself through the eyes of others, and she liked what she saw.

Malika felt as if there were more light, more beauty, more kindness. And though she knew the admiration of a layperson was worth little, Götz's enthusiasm did her good. He was endlessly impressed by her violin playing. He listened when she practiced, looked at the music on her stand, and said with a shake of his head, *How do you find your way around all that chaos?*

The time of being alone was over. Boosted by the power of his love, her best qualities effortlessly came to the fore.

Later she had to admit she'd thrown all caution to the wind. When she introduced him to her parents for the first time, the recent slight from her mother paled into insignificance against the happiness she now felt in her life.

She actually did believe that just for once she had an advantage over her sister. Neither Viktoria nor Helmut took Jorinde's boyfriend Torben particularly seriously. Malika had also been present for his introduction to the Noth family. It began with the inauspicious announcement that Torben came from an antiauthoritarian household. As if choreographed, Helmut and Viktoria turned to each other with raised eyebrows and smiled.

After a dinner during which Torben lectured them all about living environmentally correctly—in itself sufficient to lose Helmut's sympathy—he tested the boundaries even further. He claimed that under a rogue regime like the GDR he would have been a resistance fighter.

Helmut gave a resounding laugh. Then he got up, shuffled to the music room shaking his head, and, without saying another word, began to practice the cello part of the *Schubert Trio in E-flat major*, which he planned to play as part of a home concert.

He didn't emerge for the rest of the evening, and Viktoria washed down her anger with red wine.

Recalling this scene, Malika was certain she could do nothing wrong with Götz.

That afternoon he called while he was out and about.

He asked what Viktoria's favorite flowers were and what Helmut liked to drink and appeared soon afterward with a bunch of hydrangeas and a heavy Spanish red wine. For the first time she saw him in a white shirt and jacket, and again Malika wondered how this man could have become her boyfriend.

As they cycled together through the park they had a lively discussion about a book they'd both read: *The Power of Positive Thinking*. While Götz talked about the passages that had most impressed him, it struck her that they'd better keep it quiet from her parents.

Helmut's voice came through the intercom.

Hello? he said.

It's us, Malika said.

What do you mean "us"? Helmut asked.

Götz and me, Papa.

Oh! That's today?

Before she could respond she heard him call out into the apartment, *Vicky! Malika's here. With her boyfriend.* Then came silence.

A few seconds later the buzzer sounded.

Helmut was standing in the doorway. *Come on in, then,* he muttered.

As he went on ahead he said, *So you're a furniture restorer! We've got a couple of things with minor defects.*

I'd be very happy to take a look, Götz said.

Viktoria shot out of the kitchen and opened her arms wide. *Welcome!* she said. Normally she did all the housework in her best clothes, but today she was wearing an apron. It was spotless and the creases were clearly visible. She must have only just taken it out of the packet.

The improvised supper consisted of tomato salad with too much onion, toast, and scrambled eggs. *Wonderful eggs,* Helmut said, smacking his lips.

Götz put on a brave face. She saw the apathy in her parents' eyes, then looked at the magnificent flowers and the expensive wine and felt surges of disappointment and pity.

*

The first and only meeting with both sets of parents took place when Malika and Götz had been together for not quite a year. The date had been postponed three times, on each occasion because of Viktoria and Helmut.

Götz and Malika fetched his parents from the hotel and walked to the restaurant. Only a few days before, as a joke, Helmut had threatened to laugh the moment the Swabians mentioned *money* or *saving*. And so Malika had thought it a safer that they meet on neutral ground.

The stroll from the hotel to the restaurant took them past Nicolaikirche and Thomaskirche. Malika talked about Felix Mendelssohn Bartholdy, who played a key role in reviving interest in Bach—rather forgotten at the time—and was the first to make an endowment toward a statue of the composer. Visiting this oldest Bach statue would involve only a short detour, but Götz's father looked at his watch and said, *Well, I'm hungry now.* Nodding in agreement, his mother tucked her arm into her husband's, and that was that.

During the introductions, Götz's father made it clear that *he* was going to treat them all to dinner, and after drinks had been ordered and dishes chosen, he said with peculiar pride in his voice that he and his wife had been to the old East Germany only twice, today being the second time.

Once for every decade of reunification, Helmut said, then turned to Viktoria and asked, *How often have we been to the West, Vicky? Seventy, eighty times?*

Viktoria threw her hair back in an exaggerated gesture and began counting out loud. *It must have been a hundred and twenty times*, she said. She smiled and the tiny lines around her green eyes looked so pretty that Malika felt a twinge. Götz's mother replied quickly, *Well, we've got some catching up to do, then.*

They spent the rest of the evening talking past each other.

While Viktoria doggedly tried to lend the conversation a certain depth by embarking on particular topics, Götz's parents talked about their three other children. They chatted about a recently born grandchild, the renovation of their house, and the advantages and disadvantages of cars less than a year old. Helmut was already bored during the appetizer. He shuffled his feet restlessly, went outside several times to smoke, and engaged Götz in a bizarre conversation about woodworm.

Viktoria felt she had to talk about her daughters, too. But principally she reeled off Jorinde's achievements: their sweet granddaughter, Ada; Jorinde's latest role in a television film; and all the other offers she had to choose from. At the mention of the TV film, Götz's mother pricked up her ears. She'd seen it and a touch of obsequiousness briefly crept into her behavior.

Helmut and Viktoria exchanged meaningful glances.

Malika was in no doubt that Götz's mother's existence as a housewife, her awe of a television actress, and her ignorance about the East would be rich fodder for Helmut and Viktoria to chew over for half the night. And to make things worse, Götz's father frequently dropped the word *money* into conversation. The mockery and teasing of others had always united her parents.

Götz seemed to have sensed her tension. He placed a hand on her neck and a pleasant shudder ran down her spine.

With him around nothing could happen to Malika. The influence of her parents ended where his love began.

She pops into her mother's preferred florist's. With her violin on her back, her bag over her shoulder, and an armful of beautiful hydrangeas she makes her way through the late summer afternoon. Sweat runs between her breasts and down her back. She hates the dusty heat of the waning season, she hates the dryness and shriveled leaves, the scorched grass and the tiredness of all life. The plane trees that line the way are shedding their old bark on a large scale. Their trunks stand bright and unprotected, and a searing wind swirls around prematurely fallen leaves. Screwing up her eyes, Malika turns into the music quarter.

Vicky will be glowing, even though she's not as beautiful as she once was. Nobody calls her by her nickname anymore. She has long since smoked and drunk away her claim to be *Beauty*. Her despair at the decay manifests itself in the bathroom.

There is a cream for every single part of her body, and an additional serum for the particularly tricky areas, such as around her eyes. Algae extracts, hyaluronan, aloe vera, and vitamin A are there to bolster and nourish Viktoria's thin, almost translucent skin. Malika is moved by the care and time she allocates to her withering body. Behind the jars and pots of these expensive cosmetics lives fear. Her mother is fragile too.

Helmut doesn't appear to be worried about getting old.

On the shelf above his sink are a mug with his toothbrush, a dish with shaving soap, a shaving brush, and a wet razor. His plump face is almost devoid of wrinkles.

Malika opens the door to the building.

Since her parents fell ill she's had her own key. She presses a button to call the lift, which comes down to meet her behind the wrought-iron art nouveau cage. The rooms upstairs are not the same as those in which she grew up. When the building was renovated, the huge apartments were divided up. For three years her parents lived a few streets away, then returned to their scaled-down apartment with a tenfold rent increase.

In the lift she braces herself and thinks of the image the psychotherapist gave her as a takeaway from their last session. In it she wears an invisible protective suit that keeps out anything that harms her, while letting through everything that's benign.

She opens their door with her key and goes in.

* * *

Was there anything lovelier than this moment?

She was in the kitchen, cooking.

The evening light slanted through the west-facing window and onto the set table. Cloth napkins lay on the plates, the water carafe with gemstones was full.

Then his key in the door, his footsteps in the hallway. She didn't turn around. She waited for his hands to touch her shoulders, to sweep her hair to one side, and for him to kiss the back of her neck.

There was nothing more lovely than this moment.

They'd been a couple for more than two years, and for around eighteen months had been living in the sunny three-room apartment, not far from the shop and the workshop.

The imbalance in their love didn't bother Malika. From the very first moment her feelings for Götz had been unwavering.

She'd been the driving force behind their first few meetings. She had decided when they should move in together.

At the same time, they didn't share everything.

Götz could appreciate classical music only on an emotional level. He read travelogues and books about alternative life-forms, but he didn't know a single great work of literature. His cleverness was different from the type Malika was familiar with at home. It was based on experience, perception, and what he'd picked up in his journeyman years.

In bed he wanted to do things she didn't like. And he wanted her often and fiercely. Not even her periods stopped him from exploring her body in broad daylight. His curiosity made her freeze, and she felt ashamed at the desires he articulated out loud.

She preferred to have him take her in the soft evening light, silently and with her eyes closed. When his breathing quickened and his entire body tensed, then she, too, made a few sounds of pleasure.

In her relationship with Götz the urge to have a child became a powerful instinct, further intensified when Jorinde got there first.

In the shop she found the child's bed, which had come from an old Bavarian farmhouse. She stroked with both hands the curved headboard, painted with gentians and edelweiss, and when Götz wrapped his arms around her from behind and asked, *What are you thinking?* she said, *Our child will sleep in this bed*. Instead of replying he laughed, took her hand, and led her into the workshop.

*

Two years later the bed was still in the same place. Everyone could see it from the pavement through the display window. Several customers had asked the price and Götz had always given the same answer: *It's not for sale*.

In the meantime, every visit to the bathroom at the end of her monthly cycle had become fraught with anxiety, every tugging in her abdomen a sign of imminent disappointment. And whenever Malika's hopes for a child were again drowned in menstrual blood, she would lie in bed for hours with the curtains drawn.

So it was on that humid summer's day too.

Early in the evening she heard, as ever, his footsteps in the hallway. She took the dish of baked eggplant out of the oven, put down the oven mitts, lit a match, and held it to the wick of the candle on the table. In a few seconds his beard would scratch the back of her neck and his warm lips would caress her skin. This would ease the pain.

He put his head in the doorway to say *Hello*, then went past the kitchen to the bathroom.

Malika turned around.

She looked at the shoes that he'd carelessly left in the middle of the hallway. The bathroom door was locked. Water was running; she stood there silently and listened.

When the rushing of the water stopped, she hurried back into the kitchen. He came in soon after, but instead of the usual display of affection he merely gave her a fleeting kiss on the cheek.

Over supper Götz mentioned that another customer had shown an interest in the bed and told her how a storm broke just as he gave his usual reply: *It's not for sale.* He even remembered the name of the young woman and smiled and shook his head when he said it: *Brida Lichtblau.*

Her pulse accelerated, her mouth turned dry, and her vision narrowed to his facial expressions, his look. She was gripped by a dreadful fear.

Not long after that evening, when she was changing the sheets, Malika came across a packet of condoms in the gap between the bedframe and the mattress. They hadn't been using protection for a long time as both wanted children. Nothing was more important to Malika, and so without hesitation she threw the condoms away.

That same evening Götz looked for them.

He needed a break from the pressure to conceive, he explained crossly. He felt they weren't sleeping with each other for pleasure anymore, but only with the aim of getting pregnant.

Again Malika was seized by anxiety. And she was tormented by the suspicion that something else lay behind his behavior.

She said nothing when he began to take more care with the way he dressed.

She said nothing when his trips away became more frequent and longer, and he wasn't hungry for her on his return.

And when he started putting his phone on silent and always carrying it with him at home, she didn't ask why.

Nightmares dragged her into dark worlds.

When she awoke she felt sick with fear.

She couldn't lose Götz.

✳ ✳ ✳

Malika!

Viktoria hurries over and hugs her. The hint of alcohol on her breath mingles with the reek of a recent cigarette. She takes the flowers, sticks her nose into a cluster, inhales exaggeratedly, and runs into the kitchen.

There is a manageable number of guests. Some usual faces are missing.

Those are the people who always struggled with Helmut's way of thinking. The anger when he posed his heretical questions had always been huge.

Is the late-capitalist, Western-liberal social order really the best system? he would toss into a cheerful conversation. *Should every idiot be allowed the vote? What do you think of a wise king?*

Anyone who declined to debate along such lines would be accused by Helmut of being *small-minded*, *anti-intellectual*, or *vapid*, depending on the degree of their refusal. But it was only when the media lashed into eastern Germany, criticizing the people for taking democracy literally, that the split among their friends led to a number of them breaking off contact. Helmut doesn't mince his words with those who have remained.

Malika spots Ruth, Viktoria's best friend, and her husband Karl-Ursus, the Serbian clarinetist Milovan with his wife, Una, and the Russian violinist Vasily with his entire family. She greets the Polish viola player Agata, the music editor Viola Lenz, and Rüdiger, now gray. Nobody calls him Roofing-Felt-Rudi anymore.

In the music room is a small group of nice people. An immaculately dressed man with rimless spectacles, his face devoid of any remarkable features, offers her his hand.

Very pleased to meet you, he says, introducing himself as Bertram Weisshaupt.

She feels a shudder. His voice is like Götz's. She listens attentively as he tells her how much he enjoyed the evening of chamber music with Schubert string quartets in the Gohlis Palace. Malika was one of the performers. She seems to have made an impression on him and he clearly understands something about music.

While Viktoria circulates with a tray of sekt glasses, Bertram

Weisshaupt goes on talking. Occasionally he touches his spectacles with his left index finger and smiles sheepishly. There is something gauche about his posture; he stands as if doubled up. He certainly wouldn't make impositions on her several times a week with his sex drive. Perhaps this man with slim arms and legs is the best thing that could happen to her.

When her father suggests they continue their conversation at the table, she follows them into the kitchen and takes a seat beside Bertram.

✳ ✳ ✳

She waited on a porch.

Residents came and went. Some eyed her suspiciously, others held the door open for her or asked who she'd come to see.

She didn't let the shop out of her sight. Once Götz came outside with two men and shook hands with them before going straight back inside. Then nothing happened for a long time.

Twice before she'd spent half an afternoon waiting on various porches. On the first occasion it was the rain that caused her to give up, on the second it was her dignity.

This time nothing was going to stop her.

Götz came out before he usually shut up shop. Dressed in a fresh set of clothes, he hung the CLOSED sign on the door, brought his old bike inside, and appeared seconds later with the racer over his shoulder. He leaned it against the wall, put the leather clip that Malika had given him for his birthday around his right trouser leg, got on the bike, and rode off.

Malika struggled to keep up with his pace. Twice she crossed roads riskily to avoid losing him.

She followed him down Giesserstrasse and Karl-Heine-Strasse, hared after him down Josephstrasse as far as Linde-nauer Markt, and finally saw him disappear into a building diagonally opposite Nathanaelkirche.

To the rear of the church, between two dense bushes and a wall, she looked for somewhere to wait.

Around an hour and a half later he left the building accompanied by a woman.

Although they didn't touch each other, they stood very close and stared into each other's eyes. Then they unlocked their bicycles from a lamppost and rode off their separate ways. Both turned around one final time and waved.

The woman was wearing a colorful, flowery A-line skirt and a low-cut black top. Her dark-blond hair was in crown plaits. Her body was firm and compact, her movements springy. When she stood up on the pedals, her hips moved lithely from side to side.

The woman stopped outside a chemist's. She leaned the bicycle against a wall, took her mobile from her handbag, read a message, and smiled. Then she typed something herself, put the phone back into her bag, and entered the shop.

She spent time looking at the face creams, opting for an expensive organic product, then went to the hair care section, where she put a hair oil she seemed to know into the basket. She also picked up a bag of mixed nuts and two bars of dark chocolate.

At the checkout, Malika put a packet of chewing gum as

well as the exact change for it on the conveyor belt and stood so close behind the woman that she could see the tiny blond hairs on the back of her neck. With her firm, narrow shoulders and slightly hollow back she looked like an overextended bow.

Would you like a receipt? the checkout lady said.

No, thanks, I don't need it, the woman said. Her voice was rough and deep.

Malika watched her pack the items into a black cloth bag, which said WASH BAG on it, sweep a few recalcitrant hairs from her forehead, and leave the shop with short, capricious steps.

No doubt she was one of those women Götz usually described as high maintenance and yet felt attracted to. Women who were so in need of attention that they didn't exist without it, that even a visit to the supermarket turned into a stage performance.

Once outside, she put the cloth bag into the pannier, got on the bike, and pedaled away.

Malika wheeled her bicycle. She would have to beg off from her chamber orchestra rehearsal that evening. She would also call in sick to the music school. It was impossible to tell what was going to happen in the next few days.

She climbed the steps to her apartment, opened the door, stepped into the hallway, and stood still.

Götz came out of the bathroom.

I thought you were teaching, he said, giving her a peck on the cheek. A towel was around his neck and his hair was wet. He didn't avoid her gaze.

Everything O.K.? he asked, rubbing his hair dry.

Malika moved closer to him and to her astonishment said, *I'm pregnant.*

* * *

Bertram holds a hand over his glass. His fingers are long and thin.

Oh, come on! Viktoria says insistently. She's suspicious of people who don't drink. Looking slightly bemused and after a brief fiddle with his spectacles, Bertram mutters, *Just a sip, then.*

Satisfied, Viktoria fills half the glass with wine and Bertram goes on talking about how naïve the federal government is to believe that the mass of poorly educated immigrants, often insufficiently literate even in their own mother tongue, will generate our pensions in the future.

His factual knowledge is extensive; not even Helmut can follow him. Malika sees the strain in the corners of her father's mouth, which twitch and droop, then refocuses her gaze on Bertram.

Unlike Götz he merely stirs a cool interest in her, mixed with a faint skepticism. Her father's new friends have one thing in common: they hold forth and rarely ask questions. Their minds appear to be shut, they seem to have definite answers to almost everything. She doesn't know how her father fits in, as he's never trusted people who are too sure of themselves.

She listens for a while, then runs through in her mind what she intends to say to Jorinde later. She'll start with the *No!* to the child. From there she'll set out all the injustices she's had to put up with from her parents because of Jorinde. And right at the end she'll say, *Why don't you ask Viktoria? She knows all about getting rid of children.*

It's a pain that won't go away.

Less than three weeks after Malika was born, Viktoria and Helmut took her with a suitcase full of clothes and nappies to Viktoria's mother in the Ore Mountains. Malika spent the whole first year of her life with her grandmother. Viktoria carried on with her studies and supposedly visited her baby as often as she could. If her grandmother is to be believed, this happened every three months, so four times in total. After she returned to her parents, Malika was dropped off at the daycare facility at six o'clock every morning and picked up at six in the evening.

The premature Jorinde, by contrast, was breastfed for six months and not once entrusted to anyone else's care during that time.

Malika's *No!* will contain this and much more besides.

Excuse me for a moment. Helmut gets up and goes to the bathroom with his typical shuffle. Malika watches him, hoping he'll be back quickly.

I admire artists like you and your father, Bertram says, *but I'm an economist. I feel more at home in the world of facts and figures.*

I'm not an artist, Malika says. *I'm a craftswoman of my instrument.*

The distinction was important to her even when she was with Götz. He bridged the gap and put their jobs on an equal footing.

That's interesting, Bertram says and launches into a lecture on art as mankind's tutor. His talk keeps branching out until

Malika can no longer follow. She nods, smiles, and thinks of Götz, picturing his handsome face before her. No effort was necessary with him. She was able just to love him.

✳ ✳ ✳

When the magic word had faded away Malika could still hear it. The word had fallen from her lips, but she'd had nothing to do with it.

Pregnant? Götz said.

Yes, she said.

But we've been using contraception.

Yes, she said, *but sometimes it happens anyway.*

He nodded silently, took her in his arms, and held her tightly.

✳

For a while he came back home at the usual time. He was friendly and caring, albeit quiet and pensive.

The pregnancy was a good cover for her frequent tears. Even her affection could easily be attributed to her hormones.

The child seemed to be the salvation for their relationship.

Only there was no child, and in the hope of transforming her lies into reality Malika slept with him almost every day.

On the day her period began Götz left the apartment early to organize the transport and construction of a wardrobe. Over breakfast he'd raved about traditional assembly techniques. Nineteenth-century furniture could be put together without a single screw. She'd been half listening to him enthuse about *grooves* and *wedges* when the familiar tugging in her womb began.

As soon as the door to their apartment closed she lay on the bed and closed her eyes. She could feel the blood flowing out of her in waves, running warm down her buttocks and seeping into the sheets.

Later she took the tram to see her gynecologist. On the pavement outside the building she called Götz and asked him to pick her up.

Back home, he changed the bedclothes, made some tea, and sat beside her. *It'll be fine next time*, he said. *A miscarriage isn't anything unusual.*

＊

He began to get home later in the evenings again, and his trips became extended. On more than one occasion Malika was close to confronting him, but the saving grace of love lay in the ability to turn a blind eye. Helmut had done the same: looked away and kept quiet.

While Götz was cheating on her Malika kept putting on weight, and each time she looked in the mirror her hatred for the other woman grew. One illness seamlessly followed another. Suffering became an everyday experience.

One night Malika was woken by a crashing sound. Götz lay in the hallway, blind drunk. He'd fallen against the shoe cabinet and was groaning.

He spent the rest of the night on the floor by the toilet. From time to time he pulled himself up and hung his head over the bowl until nothing more came out. She cleaned the toilet lid and wiped any traces of vomit from his face with a wet flannel.

Götz slept through the next day, and in the evening Malika felt as if she'd awoken from a dream. She stood in the bedroom with her back to the open window. Everything felt close and genuine. The fog that had engulfed her for so long had vanished.

Götz looked at her and stretched out an arm. In his eyes she could see gratitude.

Y

The following weeks were far too happy.

Since it was summer vacation, the shop was open for only a few hours each day and he didn't do anything in the workshop. They slept in every morning and had breakfast together, and in the afternoons they cycled to Kulkwitzer See and swam across to the other side. On a sloping meadow with apple trees they lay naked in the evening sun, speaking again about things that lay in the future.

The affair was over.

She was certain of it.

*

On their last evening together, Götz put a large hunk of meat on the table.

Can you cook this? he said. *It's venison. Freshly killed.*

Where did you get it? Malika asked, unwrapping the meat from the waxy paper.

A customer, he said, heading for the bathroom.

Roe or red deer?

Red deer, I think.

You don't know?

No.

She hesitated. The Götz she knew would have asked the customer. He would have listened to the story of the hunt in its entirety and asked for details.

When she picked up the meat with both hands, she could feel that it was still frozen on the inside. It couldn't be freshly killed, as he claimed.

Her pulse quickened.

The only way she knew of preparing venison was to roast it with a red wine sauce and lingonberries. She sent Götz back out to get the ingredients. He put on his dark-green parka, slipped his wallet into his back trouser pocket, and stepped into the stairwell. Then he stopped and came back for his mobile phone, which was on the hall table.

Her mind couldn't draw any rational connection between the meat and the telephone, but her instinct raised the alarm and she felt a cramping in her stomach as she had when it first began.

She laid her warm hands around the meat. The icy center was thawing. A thin, red trickle dripped from the edge of the table and onto her dress. All her thoughts were pushing in the same direction. And at the end of every thought was an image.

She wouldn't be able to turn a blind eye again.

Her gaze landed on the clock on the wall. He ought to have been back long ago. The shop was less than five hundred yards away. She stood up, wiped her hands on her dress, took a knife from the block, and stabbed the blade into the meat. Again and again.

By the time he came back it was dark.

Malika was sitting in silence on her chair.

I'm sorry, he said, *but I can't go on like this.*

* * *

Bertram is talking insistently to her father. His face, which to begin with Malika thought was featureless, now looks gritty and determined.

Since Helmut came back from the bathroom, Bertram hasn't shown any discernible interest in her.

She looks up at Viktoria, who's leaning against the doorframe beside Ruth. Malika catches a few words: names of classical singers and musicians. They're probably talking about the last Handel festival; Viktoria had gone to almost every concert.

Let's ask my daughter, Helmut says suddenly, slamming his hand on the table. *Do men and women each have a natural purpose? In a reordering of society this question needs to be addressed.*

Malika smiles. Not even Bertram can avoid Helmut's pet topic.

What reordering of society? she says, to win time.

The one that is imminent, Bertram says, coming to Helmut's defense. *The dictatorship of the moralists won't last forever. The world is becoming more conservative once more, and men and women will have to assume distinct roles.*

If everything had turned out the way she wanted . . .

But that's not what happened.

Turning to Helmut, she says a touch too harshly, *Rubbish! What natural purpose are you talking about?*

When your Swabian handyman was still on the scene you talked differently, Helmut retorts.

And? she says. *What do you want to do with childless women like me? Shove us into a nunnery? Forced marriage?*

Her father laughs. *Why not?* he says, taking a large gulp of wine. Bertram shakes his head vigorously. *No,* he says, *that's not what we mean. It's about the differences we ought to acknowledge and the limits of our own autonomy.*

Malika also rejects the idea that an individual can shape themselves and the world at will, but as she's searching for the right words a phone goes off. Bertram feels in the inner pocket of his jacket. He declines the call and places the mobile on the table. The lock screen shows a Doberman with a shining coat.

At that moment Jorinde enters the kitchen.

Malika can feel the tension drain from her body.

Helmut gets up. He opens his arms wide and waits for Jorinde to embrace him. *My kitten,* he says in his sweet voice, peering past her into the hallway. But neither Torben nor the children are there. Jorinde has come on her own.

For a moment Malika closes her eyes and sticks to her therapist's advice. Instead of comparing herself to Jorinde, she gauges herself against her former self. She sees how much she's developed, what she's achieved, that she's become a popular violin teacher.

Only then does she get to her feet and walk tall over to her sister.

Jorinde is sitting on the balcony. On her own. Malika could have followed her sister, but the conversation with Bertram had turned interesting. As the invitees start to crowd around the canapés in the kitchen she goes to the bathroom. She locks the door and sits on the rim of the bathtub. Bertram definitely smiled at her when she pushed her way past the hungry guests. They seem to be closer mentally than she'd expected. Tongue-in-cheek, she'd summed up the points on which they agreed. *Not everything new is good. Not every foreigner comes in peace. Not every border is restrictive.* He nodded in relief, then she got up from the table.

Still, he can't hold a candle to Götz.

When she was discharged from the psychiatric clinic one cold, sunny November day, she was able to see the future clearly ahead of her.

Vicky and Helmut were waiting beside a covered grand piano and an oasis of tropical houseplants. Patients sat limply in the yellow fake-leather armchairs dotted all over the place, gawping at their smartphones. Malika went down the stairs, one by one, thinking that from this point onward her life was going to be a hopeless search. She wouldn't be able to love in the same way again. And she didn't want to love any less.

After the move, she was helped by a steady rhythm of work, therapy, and organized activities in her free time. In the two summers that followed she even went occasionally to the lake, to the sloping meadow with its apple trees. She swam to the other side and back. She didn't see Götz once. At a time when the memories no longer weighed down every grain of present happiness like lead, she saw the display stand outside her local bookshop. The woman on the picture was Brida Lichtblau. The title of her book was *Life Patterns*.

On the evening of the book launch Malika felt sure she'd see him. In the front row, watching proudly as his wife sat at the table and read. She scanned the seats. To the right she recognized Dr. Gabriel and next to her the bookseller with the red hair. Götz was missing.

She looked around again. He wasn't there.

Malika barely caught anything about the contents of the book. Her thoughts wouldn't keep still. His absence could mean anything, and that *anything* included the possibility they could try again. But Brida's words at the end of the reading shattered her hopes. She thanked her husband, Götz, who sadly couldn't be there that evening because their young daughter was ill.

The following morning Malika cycled to the shop and squinted through the display window. The bed had gone. She continued on to the bookshop and bought herself a copy of *Life Patterns.*

Since then she's read everything Brida Lichtblau has written. Every male character has some of Götz's features. She doesn't get any closer to him.

According to the bookseller, Malika is Brida's biggest fan.

She stands in front of the mirror, puts her hair up into a high, loose bun, and applies some lipstick. It has to have an end. She knows this.

Through the frosted glass of the door Malika can see someone standing outside the bathroom. One last check in the mirror then she steps into the hall.

Let's go into the bedroom, she tells Jorinde. *Nobody will bother us there.*

She stops beside the Jorinde shrine. It's stuffed with small cardigans and onesies from her first year, her first pair of shoes, her favorite doll, Lilli, various cuddly toys, a small cloth bag of marbles, and a shoebox with exercise books, pictures, and essays from her later years at school.

Viktoria has comprehensively erased the mementos of Malika's childhood. There are no baby clothes or toys, merely a few drawings and letters from her primary school days and two certificates acknowledging her participation in minor violin competitions.

Have you thought a bit more about it? Jorinde says, looking at her anxiously.

How small her sister is. Her presence onstage and the screen has nothing to do with her physical attributes. It's much more an outward projection of her inner self-confidence.

And yes. She has thought about it.

Malika has spent entire nights playing out concrete scenarios. Wondering what she would do if Jorinde demanded her child back. Imagining what the child would do if later it found out that its aunt was in fact its mother. Even picturing the reactions of her parents, colleagues, and friends. And every image, every response was a compelling argument against Jorinde's plan.

Nonetheless Malika has felt the painful urge to raise this child as her own.

Jorinde sits on the edge of their parents' bed, buries her face in her hands, and cries. The sobbing comes from deep inside, her body is shuddering.

Malika looks down at her silently. She's not going to be taken in by these stage tears. How often has she witnessed her sister's theatrical performances? Jorinde rubs her puffy eyes and wipes the snot on the sleeve of her dress.

At least sit down next to me, she says.

A few seconds later they're sitting side by side in silence.

My marriage is over, Jorinde says flatly, *and you're still furious with me.* She looks at Malika. *You ought to be angry with our parents, not me. I was just a child. Your little sister.*

Then she puts her head in Malika's lap and reaches for her hand.

Tears are running down Malika's face. She glances at the

door. They don't have much time. Viktoria will soon come looking for them.

What's happening here is a beginning, but she doesn't know
what of. *Give me a few days*, she says. *I'll come to Berlin and
then we'll talk.*

PART FIVE

Jorinde

J orinde puts her finger on the bell.

She turns up the corners of her mouth and widens her eyes. She knows how to produce an inner radiance. Now she just has to maintain it until she gets to the third floor.

The buzzer sounds, she runs up the steps, taking two at a time. The door to the apartment upstairs is ajar. When her mother comes toward her in the hallway, Jorinde opens her arms, rushes forward, and says in her deepest and most assured voice, *Happy Birthday, Vicky!*

It was less than three hours ago that Torben put his face right up to hers and yelled that she was completely mad. Ill, crazy, nuts. Only someone from a troubled family could come up with an idea like that. When he was finished with his rant, he gasped wearily that she could go to see her batty mother and Nazi father on her own. He and the children were staying in Berlin.

Jorinde went.

She was utterly absent as she sat in the tram to the railway station and was on autopilot as she made her way through the station and down the escalator to the deep-level platforms 1 and 2. All the way to Leipzig she stared out of the window instead of learning the script for her forthcoming TV appearance. Just a minor role in an episode of a crime series, but still.

As the familiar landscape drifted past she decided on illness as the excuse for her family not being there. Then her thoughts turned to what she had to discuss with Malika.

Where are my sweeties?

Viktoria takes a step backward. Her expression is a combination of doubt and reproach. Without hesitating, Jorinde tells her about a rampant virus at the school, embellishing her story with gruesome details that, as expected, stifle Viktoria's interest.

Malika is sitting at the kitchen table with their father and another man. Although Jorinde doesn't know him, one look is enough. Boring. Helmut gets up. *My kitten,* he says when she gives him a hug. And for a second time the virus story stands in for the unpleasant truth that her marriage is over and she's pregnant for a third time.

When, soon afterward, the soft arms of her sister close around her, Jorinde just wants to cry.

For as long as she can remember she has fought for Malika's love.

How often did she stand outside her sister's locked bedroom door, kicking it angrily when yet again Malika hissed, *Go away, I've got to practice!* Then she would run to her mother to be comforted, and to say bad things about Malika.

The look on her sister's face tells her that she hasn't changed her mind. Still, it's worth one last try.

Only a society that values community above the individual is resilient, the colorless man beside Malika says.

The GDR was a great example of that, Malika remarks ironically.

There were other reasons for the failure of the GDR, he objects. *The peaceful revolution—.*

It wasn't a peaceful revolution, Helmut interrupts. *It was a capitalist restoration. The people sold their soul to consumerism and nobody protected them from it.*

The big topics, as ever. Helmut can't help himself. Jorinde gazes out at the neighboring park where they used to go and feed the squirrels. Some were so trusting they would eat out of her hand. On one such occasion Malika clapped her hands, sending the animal scurrying away. Jorinde wept bitterly and Malika wasn't allowed to go to the pool for a week, even though swimming was her favorite hobby at the time.

Around the table they're talking about immigration. Thank goodness Torben is far away. He would say things she'd be ashamed of, and Helmut would smile indulgently. Torben lacks all political sense and Helmut's lenience toward him only makes it worse.

The differences in opinion between her and her family have narrowed. She's no longer an antifascist activist, on account of which Torben called her *opportunistic, mousy,* and *cowardly.*

Vicky darts around, filling people's glasses without asking. She won't be satisfied until most of the guests are as plastered as she is. In spite of the makeup, her nose is shimmering red. Her mother has been drinking too much for many years. She's suffering from the visible effects of this and she keeps drinking to forget the fact.

Daniela Krien

You're standing all on your own, she says, and scolds Helmut, urging him to include his daughter. But Jorinde doesn't want to join them; she has no desire to get involved in a political discussion.

To begin with she, too, was disconcerted by the change in Helmut's views, which Vicky largely endorses. The tolerance of her friends and colleagues ends in the center of the political spectrum. They're left-leaning liberals and cosmopolitan, which inevitably produces an abhorrence of nationalism and isolation. The mantralike repetition of their high moral stance suppresses the doubts that nonetheless stir.

At first she didn't take her parents' newfound conservatism seriously. A generational conflict, no more and no less. But now, when she considers it more closely, Helmut's and Vicky's volte-face doesn't appear quite so contradictory. They never shared the optimistic narrative of progress that took hold in the 1990s after the GDR joined with the West unconditionally. Maybe back then Jorinde had been closer to her parents than she'd assumed. These days she can't position herself anywhere anymore. While Torben feels at home with the far left, she's searching in vain for her own home.

Jorinde wouldn't marry Torben a second time. She met him when she was working at one of the indie theaters in Berlin. There was an immediate spark. The inner turmoil that drove him haunted her, too. The fear of missing out on something important ensured that they were always among the first to get drunk, and the last to leave a party. And yet their hunger for life was never sated.

They drank, had sex, smoked packet after packet of cigarettes, and often turned up to rehearsals late. Contact with her parents was restricted to Vicky's occasional phone calls. Jorinde would then speak—at a pace that allowed no room for questions—about how fabulous her life in the theater was, how close she was to making a breakthrough, and how extraordinarily talented her boyfriend was. It was what Vicky wanted to hear, and what she could broadcast to others afterward. Malika had already taken on the role of the problem child.

Helmut was patronizing toward Torben from day one, but Jorinde stuck resolutely with him. The most significant reason for this was the tiny thing in her tummy, which was less than an inch long on the day Torben first met her parents and nobody yet knew about it.

Ada was the emergency brake. Jorinde quit smoking from one day to the next. She stopped drinking and calmed the waves that in the past had tossed her hither and thither. When she met Vera on the panting course, which is what Torben disparagingly called the prenatal classes, her hedonistic days were numbered too. Vera's casting agency became Jorinde's springboard into film.

Torben kept on going as before. Only Ada's appearance as a tangible, audible entity kept him on the straight and narrow for a while, and in the confidence of that phase they got married.

Later, however, when his age and the children required him to adapt his desires to reality, he refused to bend. He rarely compromised, and certainly not at a professional level. His tactlessness disguised as honesty cost him countless friendships and career opportunities.

She still defends Torben against her parents. Nobody readily admits to a mistake like that. *What a windbag!* Helmut said after the first meeting, and his assessment of Torben was reconfirmed time after time.

Her husband is a child, almost six feet three inches tall, who despite all his faults wants to be loved unconditionally. But she's not his mother.

Until now she's kept the whole truth about the state of her marriage from her sister, too.

Out of the corner of her eye she watches Malika and the man with the cold eyes. The fine curve of his lips is in strange contrast to the upper part of his face. The longer she looks at him, the more striking he appears. If Jorinde felt like it, she could make him shift his attention toward her, but she doesn't even fancy doing that.

She needs to talk to Malika. Time is pressing and their last telephone conversation ended on a sour note. *Why doesn't Torben care about his offspring?*

Because it's not his.

Malika's tone became harsh. *How could that happen? Haven't you heard of contraception?*

And Jorinde asked rudely whether she'd never been in a situation where lust had gotten the better of her. Malika hung up without saying another word.

The smokers come in from the balcony, led by Roofing-Felt-Rudi.

She would never forget what Malika told her about Vicky and

Rüdiger. At the time she thought her sister had fabricated the story, but now she's not so sure.

Jorinde steps out onto the balcony. The plantings are extravagant. Her mother detests geraniums and other long-flowering plants. Instead she has white agapanthus flowerheads next to purple blazing stars and sunflowers. She sits in a wicker chair and looks through the railings at the pavement below, where a woman is standing with four children.

In three weeks' time it will be too late. That's when the legal abortion limit expires. The child's father doesn't know. His wife and young daughter will keep smiling their smiles beside him in the tabloids. He's a real cliché. His name makes intelligent women abandon all dignity. His acting talent forgives everything. On a personal level he's a total loser. But what physical presence! And that's why she made a beeline for him and said *Yes!* in his hotel room when he asked if she was on the pill. She didn't want any interruptions.

An abortion would be the easier solution. But who wouldn't want a child by this man?

Things wouldn't be so bad if filming for her first major feature film weren't due to start a few weeks after the scheduled birth. She couldn't bring the tiny creature with her; it would affect the quality of her work. She needs to be free. Even though there won't be any nude scenes, her body has to be hers alone.

Torben made it clear that he would only look after Ada and Jonne. And he doesn't even know that another man is the father of this baby.

She turns around and looks through the closed balcony door. The guests are slowly gathering in the kitchen. She would really rather not go back in.

Jorinde immediately abandoned the idea of giving the baby to Vicky to look after. She remembers all too well the scenes after Ada was born.

Vicky arrived with a mountain of presents and excitedly fussed over the baby. At the same time she whined about what a difficult time she'd had herself, without the technological aids around today, without a helping hand, and with a husband who was always on tour with the orchestra and regarded changing a baby's nappy as beneath him. Then there was Malika, who was often ill and lacking in charm. Unlike Jorinde, who had been a ray of sunshine from the beginning; she did nothing but laugh for the first year of her life.

As Viktoria spoke she held tiny Ada on her arm and wandered around, rocking her hectically and wondering why the baby wouldn't stop screaming.

You're going to have a better time of it, she called to Jorinde over Ada's head. *I'll help you, I'll take the child off you so you've got some time to yourself.*

But Jorinde didn't want time to herself. She wanted to be with Ada. At the time it was still good between her and Torben; the only annoying thing was her mother.

Later, when Ada became really hard work and, egged on by Torben, developed a sullen contrariness, Vicky no longer reiterated her offer.

Jorinde asked her mother for help on precisely two occasions.

The first time, she was pregnant with Jonne. Vicky had come to Berlin for the day and they went out for an ice cream. When Ada's scoop started dripping, Jorinde pushed it down slightly into the cone. *I want the ice cream up again!* howled three-year-old Ada, completely unmoved by Jorinde's explanations that it wouldn't spill anymore now. *I want the ice cream up again!* she was still screaming when it had melted entirely and the cone had been tossed into a bin. *Could you take her to Leipzig for a few days?* Jorinde asked. Vicky glanced skeptically at Ada who'd well and truly abandoned herself to her hysteria, then uttered a determined *No.* Helmut's nerves wouldn't cope, she explained. He'd recently been diagnosed with tinnitus and Dr. Gabriel had told him he needed peace and quiet.

The second time, Ada was already a schoolchild. Having set off in the morning on her skateboard she'd fallen and broken her left arm. By chance Helmut and Vicky were in Berlin that day for a concert by the Philharmonic. Jorinde called Vicky's mobile at around 2 p.m. and asked whether she and Helmut could pop by for a couple of hours. Torben wasn't there, Ada was complaining about her plaster cast and the pain, and the fridge was empty.

Jorinde clearly heard Vicky say to Helmut, *Fracture of the forearm, four weeks in a cast. And with that temper.*

To Jorinde she said, *We'd love to help out, but time's a bit tight today.*

The first person to find out about the pregnancy was Kira. Jorinde did the test in the bathroom at a film studio and later burst into tears in full makeup. Kira listened attentively as she worked on Jorinde's puffy eyes, and when Jorinde's lips started quivering again, she said, *Stop!*

Kira gave her a searching look and lit a cigarette. *Why don't you ask your sister? Hasn't she always wanted children?*

Kira's mind knows no boundaries. Taking her advice means flouting social norms. And the more Jorinde considered her suggestion, the less ludicrous it seemed.

What did she have to lose? Her relationship with Malika was complicated, but not irretrievably broken. Their encounters on parents' birthdays and public holidays generally passed off peacefully, and in the best-case scenario her sister would regard the child as a dream come true.

The flaw in the plan was the point when Jorinde took her child back. And so the idea of a time-limited custodianship of the baby turned into one of handing the child over to Malika for good.

The balcony door flies open. *The clock doth chime, it's supper time!* Vicky calls out and laughs at her own joke. In the fairy tale "The Story of Little Muck," this is how Frau Ahavzi calls her cats at feeding time, and Vicky often used the same words to summon Malika and Jorinde to the table. Jorinde would usually come hopping and skipping, sometimes taking Malika's hand to bring her too. *Let go*, Malika would say.

Inside, the guests are thronged around the table with the canapés and salads. Malika is nowhere to be seen. She's not in the music room or sitting room, either. Jorinde waits in the hallway, staring at the bathroom door, while the guests spread out through the apartment with filled plates.

The door opens. Malika has put her hair up into a high, loose bun. She's wearing her bright-red lipstick, which she usually saves for performances. *Let's go into the bedroom*, she says. *Nobody will bother us there.*

✳ ✳ ✳

Would you open the door, Ada?

Jorinde washes her hands in the sink, dries them on a tea towel, and hurries after her daughter into the hallway.

What's for lunch, Mother? Ada says, pushing the handle down.

Please don't call me "Mother." Unless you want to wind me up.

I don't, Mother.

Jorinde takes a deep breath. Later she might need Ada's help, so she says nicely, *I haven't made your favorite dish, but there is your favorite pudding.* She looks into her daughter's defiant eyes. It's not always easy to love her. It's not easy to be fair. And the biggest challenge is to avoid abusing a mother's power.

The lift door opens in the stairwell. Malika has already taken off her rucksack and puts her things down by the door. Her face isn't giving anything away. Three days have passed since Vicky's birthday, during which time they haven't spoken. Malika hasn't wanted to.

Ada offers Malika her hand. *Hello, dear aunt*, she says in honeyed tones.

Jorinde rolls her eyes, but as so often, her hopes for an alliance with her sister are in vain.

Hello, dear niece, Malika replies. *I'm delighted to see you looking so well. I'm exhausted after the journey. Would you be so kind as to take my luggage to my quarters?*

Ada picks up the rucksack and carries it cheerfully into the guest room. It always pains Jorinde to see how well her sister gets on with the children. Not just with Ada and Jonne, but with all children. Her calm, natural authority makes education look effortless. She knows from Helmut that Malika's violin classes are heavily oversubscribed. Her pupils shine in the school concerts, and two have been placed highly in the Young Musicians competition. But even as a child Malika managed to see praise as nothing but covert criticism. Her glass is always half empty. The only period in her sister's life when this outlook on life changed was during her time with Götz.

She sets the table for everybody. Torben isn't there. Yesterday she told him that the child in her belly wasn't his and that she wanted a divorce.

He didn't seem surprised. *You'll have to pay me alimony, then*, he retorted indifferently. Until then there might still have been a small hope for their marriage.

He's staying with friends for the time being and the children don't know anything yet. She's dreading the moment when she has to tell them. At least now that Malika's here she won't have to suffer the children's pain alone.

Over lunch Jonne asks probing questions.

Where's your husband, Mali? Why don't you have any children? Don't you like children?

Tact is not innate, she'll have to teach it to him, Jorinde thinks as Malika patiently answers.

I don't have a husband, she says. *I wanted to have children, but I can't, and of course I like children. You two especially.*

Actually, my mother didn't want children, Ada pipes up. *I heard her say to Kira: Why did I have children? I must have been out of my mind.*

Jorinde senses her sister looking at her.

I didn't mean it, Ada. I was stressed.

You're always stressed.

For God's sake, Ada!

Yes, Mother?

Jorinde flings down her cutlery and leaves the room.

When she returns, Malika is explaining that mothers are people with feelings too. What she's saying is so sensible and intelligent that it almost makes Jorinde sick. Malika doesn't realize the burden. Apart from herself and her cat she has nothing to worry about. She has no idea of what day-to-day living with children is like. She doesn't know that they always fall ill at the worst moments, that they have no consideration for parents' needs, and that they demand the most attention at the most stressful times.

Now Jorinde's wondering whether it was such a good idea to get her sister to come. Whether the entire plan isn't one big mistake. Whether an abortion wouldn't be best.

Ada takes Jonne's hand and brings him to the sofa in front of the television. She doesn't want to supervise him playing with his dinosaurs so he'll have to watch the Japanese cartoon.

We'll be back in an hour, Jorinde says. She doesn't get an answer.

Malika walks upright beside her. In her heels she's almost a head taller. From Zionskirchstrasse they walk down Anklamer Strasse as far as Ackerstrasse, and from there to the Berlin Wall memorial. Malika is speaking, and what she's saying sounds sensible.

Not everything that's feasible is right. A child belongs with its mother. Jorinde needs to take responsibility, even if that means having a break from her career.

I can't afford it, she interjects angrily and cites other societies where children are brought up in larger communities without a close connection to their parents.

Malika's face says it all.

When they get to the Chapel of Reconciliation, they sit on a bench.

If Helmut had his way, we'd build another wall, Jorinde says with a bitter laugh.

Rubbish, Malika objects, *he just doesn't want to live in a consumer society.*

A group of American tourists passes by.

Consumer colonialists, Jorinde whispers conspiratorially. Malika laughs. This is the first relaxed moment between them. Jorinde leans her head on Malika's shoulder and gazes up at the evening sky.

What should I do? she says.

When they get home, Jonne runs to meet them in the hallway. *When's Papa coming home?* he says. She looks at his face, brimming with expectation. His innocence floors her. Ada comes out of the sitting room too. *Where is Papa, actually?* she asks.

Jorinde looks first at Malika, then back to the children. She wanted to do this differently—at a table, sensibly and quietly. When she utters the dreaded words, Ada's legs give way. Malika catches her just before she collapses on the floor. Jorinde takes the shaking girl from her and lifts Ada up. She offers no resistance. In a fraction of a second, the pain has changed her face.

Jonne is kneeling quietly beside them. *Why?* he asks.

The four of them sit in the hall. With tears in her eyes she tells the children that she's getting a divorce. Never has it felt better to have a sister.

It's almost midnight by the time the children are asleep. Jorinde's eyes are stinging with tiredness. Malika puts the empty wine bottle by the bin, fills the kettle, and hangs two bags of chamomile tea in a jug. Her lips are moving.

Jorinde can see her sister's hand movements, can hear sounds and words, but Malika's voice comes from far away. The sentences reach her ears, but she can't understand the meaning. Now that the deed is done, the fear comes calling. Although she doesn't love Torben anymore, she feels crushed by the children's suffering. Malika puts a cup on the table. Earthenware meets wood. Jorinde looks up.

Have you been listening to what I've been saying?

She nods, then shakes her head.

There may be a possible solution, but you'd have to come to Leipzig with the children.

Leipzig?

Yes?

When?

As soon as possible. Before the birth.

Yes, she says without thinking it over. *Let's do that.*

She meekly allows Malika to take her to bed and cover her up. And she falls asleep.

✳ ✳ ✳

Malika has spent months trawling through classified ads and asking friends. Even in Leipzig, a four-bedroom apartment with two bathrooms and a large kitchen isn't so easy to come by these days. Jorinde drags herself up the last few stairs. She thinks her belly is larger than with the other two pregnancies, yet she's still got two months to go.

Are the men at work? the real estate agent asks, letting them in.

Men? Malika says.

Jorinde smiles, looks around, and goes from room to room. There's plenty of light, enough space, and a nice atmosphere. The apartment is perfect. East–west facing, parquet floor, large rear courtyard, and a view of trees out front.

We're not going to find anything better than this, Malika whispers, now standing behind her.

I agree, Jorinde replies.

She wishes the doubts would finally go away. Her sister's dominance, Ada's refusal to go to a new school, Jonne's poor health since the separation. Each of these problems on their own is overwhelming; put together they seem insurmountable.

They agree immediately on who gets which room. That's a good sign. And when the two of them stand on the balcony,

looking down onto the courtyard, they say in unison, *Lovely!*
Jorinde contemplates the other option one last time. Without
Malika, on her own with the children. But as ever the thought
ends in chaos.

My sister and I will take the apartment, she tells the real estate agent.

You and your sister?

Yes. And our three children.

I see.

He leafs through his documents. *There are still a couple of
things that need sorting out,* he mumbles, taking a few forms
from a file. *Credit check, proof of income, and—please don't take
this the wrong way—security from your parents, maybe?*

Jorinde can see Malika's eyes darkening.

Two women and three children, he adds with a shrug. *The
owner is going to want some security.*

✳

There is a strange tension in the air.

While Vicky plays Chinese checkers with the children in
the kitchen, Helmut inspects the floor plan. He purses his lips,
wanders up and down, and seems uncomfortable.

It's a wonderful apartment, Jorinde blurts out. *The park's
right opposite and it's not too far from you and Mama, either. It's
like winning the jackpot, well, perhaps not the jackpot, but definitely the runner-up prize.* And as the words come pouring out,
Helmut lays the plan on the table and turns away. He stands

by the window with his arms crossed. His chin has sunk to his chest.

Jorinde goes quiet.

He doesn't need to spell it out. She looks to Malika for support. Her sister's face registers a serious sadness.

Why? she asks.

Why? He turns back to them. *Why? Because someone's got to bash this nonsense out of your head.*

I've resigned myself to the fact that you're going to stay on your own, he says to Malika. *But you?* He looks at Jorinde. *What sort of life are you leading? Three children who don't even have the same father! Sharing an apartment with your sister? Without a husband!* He huffs and puffs. *I'm not going to support that!*

Jorinde presses her lips together. She looks at Malika, whose face shows nothing but disbelief.

Come on! she says, pulling Malika with her.

Then she yanks open the kitchen door and calls Ada and Jonne, who are in the middle of a game and don't want to leave.

Don't ask, she hisses. *Just come. I'll explain later.*

Vicky's expression betrays no surprise.

* * *

Ada points to a stack of moving boxes. *Throw it all away*, she says. The boxes contain toys, children's books, things she's grown out of, little boxes of shells, jars with sand from the Baltic, all her dolls along with dolls' clothes, and the entire contents of her dressing-up box. As if Ada is intent on extinguishing the evidence of her childhood, as if she were embarrassed at ever having been a child.

Jorinde nods, even though later she'll make sure that all the items which have been weeded out are put in the moving van.

Jonne's bedroom looks as it always does. The floor is littered with toys. The boxes around him are empty. Whenever he's about to pack something away he starts playing with it and then forgets it needs to be packed.

Jorinde is discarding lots of things too. The best thing about moving is the opportunity to correct past excesses. Why does she need twelve pairs of jeans? What's she going to do with twenty-six fruit dishes? The cleansing effect of throwing stuff away makes it easier to deal with the chaos around her.

In the hallway her mobile vibrates.

Please call. Mama.

She can't recall the last time Vicky referred to herself as Mama. It's absurd. And of course she won't call. The last time they spoke on the phone Vicky's voice almost cracked. All because of a card.

Long live the matriarchy! Jorinde had written. She put the card in an envelope together with a copy of the tenancy agreement and sent it to her father.

They'd secured the apartment even without a security guarantee. A single telephone call to the owner had sufficed. She'd casually dropped into the conversation the name of the man whose baby she was expecting, and an invitation to the premiere of her next film probably did the rest.

After reading the card, Helmut's heart supposedly beat double time, then skipped at least three beats. He had to spend half a day in bed, Vicky said, and when Dr. Gabriel came that evening she recommended he urgently see a cardiologist. All because of her! Although they weren't able to find anything, so what did that mean? Jorinde was behaving abominably. She ought to see things from her parents' perspective. Helmut was just worried.

She really had tried to understand her father. And she knows the effect that worry can have. When recently Ada came home late and wasn't answering her mobile, first she gave her a hug, then she yelled at her and said things she'd love to be able to take back.

Helmut's concern is different, however. It's not just what her father said, but more importantly how he said it. He seemed to enjoy bashing the nonsense out of his daughters' heads. She'd heard something disconcerting in his voice, something that frightened her.

Without flagging, she continues to pack box after box and doesn't notice that Torben has come in. With an arrogant grin he drops at her feet the signed form permitting her to move with the children, officially change their address, and sign the agreements for the new schools. In the future she will need his consent for every tiny thing. Every school trip and any medical treatment will need his authorization. She won't be rid of him. Ever.

Jorinde was astonished that he gave up without a struggle. By chance she bumped into the reason for this in the foyer of the theater where she waited for him a few days earlier with the relevant documents.

She was young. So young that Jorinde felt sorry for her. But a warning would do no good. Her infatuation would make her unreceptive to the truth.

⁕

On the day of their move a group of helpers has arrived. Directed by Jorinde and spearheaded by Kira, the friends pack up the final items, supervise the children, prepare food, and clean the empty rooms. The moving van leaves Berlin late in the afternoon and early that evening Jorinde, Ada, and Jonne get to Leipzig too.

Malika has been living in the new apartment for several days. Helmut helped with her move and they met twice before that, too. Initially Jorinde was furious about this, but then she forced herself to consider the circumstances.

Malika has always run after her father. A pointless chase. Things lost too early on in life cannot be made up for now. Malika was separated from her parents for the whole of the first year of her life, and it wasn't until after Jorinde was born that Helmut realized small children need a father, too.

Although she can't feel her sister's pain, she can understand her parents' coldness.

She, too, has often left her children behind, sometimes for weeks at a time to go filming somewhere. Back home it was a nanny who was there when Ada first rode a bicycle aged three and lost the ability to speak when she got off. And it was Torben who comforted her and remained patient. On the third day her speech returned. But Jorinde wasn't there.

Every time she came home she had to win her children's trust all over again. The children didn't care that Torben spent most of the time sitting around surfing the internet, ordering pizza in the evenings, and failing to make porridge in the mornings, nor that the household was being neglected and appointments forgotten. He was there and she wasn't. Nothing else mattered. From this pain there grew a distance between her and her children. And in this distance the warmth faded.

She climbs the stairs. Ada and Jonne run past her. Upstairs Malika is standing in the doorway. It smells of roast onions and melted cheese. Jorinde embraces her sister, then crosses the threshold into another life.

✳ ✳ ✳

The first few days together pass in a busy conformity. Malika ensures that the unpacking proceeds swiftly, the fridge is full, and the apartment clean. But she takes a tactful step backward the moment it's anything to do with the children.

Soon, however, it's the children who turn to Malika. Jorinde makes the occasional feeble objection, but in truth she's grateful for all the help she can get. Before long Jonne is accompanying Malika to the music school as often as he can. After unrewarding taster sessions for piano and flute he chooses the guitar.

Now Ada will only do her homework with Malika's help. When Jorinde sees the two of them sitting with schoolbooks at the kitchen table, she tiptoes out of the room. If Ada doesn't understand something she gets into a panic. There were some awful scenes back in Berlin, and of course the anxious child didn't find studying any easier afterward. How Malika manages to explain the same thing ten times over while staying totally calm is a mystery to her.

In the evenings they sit together in the kitchen.

They take small steps forward and sometimes it feels as if they'd never lived in an apartment with the same parents. Malika's loneliness must have known no bounds.

When it gets too painful, they break off and watch films. The cinema is Malika's second home; she has reliable taste, and other people's stories mask the images of their own past.

* * *

Lilli arrives one cold April night.

No sooner had Jorinde fallen asleep than the characteristic pain began just before midnight. She's been wandering around for an hour. From the bathroom to the kitchen, down the hallway and back into the bathroom. Each time a contraction comes she grabs on to a surface for support, then moves off again.

Vicky knows and is already on her way. Malika is at the door with a packed bag. The contractions are a bearable twelve minutes apart. There's plenty of time still.

In the taxi to the hospital Malika holds her hand. Along the corridors to the labor ward she oozes calm and acts as her crutch. Malika stays with Jorinde. For every minute of the four hours. And when the midwife lays Lilli on Jorinde's chest, Malika cries.

In the weeks that follow Lilli's birth, Jonne is the only male in the household. The concentration of females generates an indefinable energy. Jorinde recovers more quickly than after the other children's births. The circle of women does her good.

She rejects Vicky's pleas to allow Helmut to visit.

Why does Malika continue to maintain contact with their father? Maybe she's had so much disappointment in the past that she can't feel any more.

As the start of shooting draws closer Jorinde contemplates chucking it all in. She doesn't want to abandon Lilli. She doesn't want the baby to have to endure the separation. This time she's got the chance to do it right. Her whole being resists the prospect of being away for weeks at a time. In retrospect, her plan of giving the child to Malika seems monstrous. Just thinking about it makes her weep, and as if she has to make amends for the idea, one afternoon she tells Malika that she won't play the role of Elsa Bruckmann.

Her sister is standing in the hallway. She and Jonne have been in town for hours, looking for a guitar for him. She's holding one shoe, the other is still on. *Are you mad?* Malika says. Jonne immediately vanishes into his room. *Where did that crazy idea come from? I thought we'd discussed all of this.*

Jorinde paces up and down with Lilli in her arms. Her eyes are fixed on the baby. *I can't leave her*, she says.

Now Malika takes off her other shoe and pulls her into the kitchen. They go on talking behind closed doors, and Jorinde can't find any response to her sister's common sense. It's true, she is skittish. Her decisions are often based on spontaneous ideas and feelings. To turn down her first major role in a feature film would be really stupid. *I've known you all my life*, Malika says, *and I know you'd regret it.*

*

On every day of filming Jorinde is woken by the ping of her telephone. Sometimes it's just Lilli in the morning photo, some times Jonne's holding her and sometimes it's Ada. Malika isn't in any of the pictures. She doesn't like being photographed.

In the evenings, too, there's always a sign from back home. Mostly Lilli is lying in the crib they've set up in Malika's bed-room while Jorinde is away.

Whenever there's a break on set she goes off to express milk, which means she can still breastfeed when she returns.

Unlike her colleagues she's not drinking and she goes to bed as early as she can. She works with greater focus than usual. The price Lilli is paying has to be justified.

Y Y Y

The windows are open. Swifts are speeding past in small groups. This is her third May in the city. Felicitas scampers toward her. She meows, looks up to see whether there's any food, then turns and goes out of the kitchen. Lilli probably frightened her out of Malika's bedroom. Lilli loves the cat. But it's not mutual.

Jorinde washes the chicken breast fillets and pats them dry with paper towels. She thinks of the good-byes at the station.

Ada just raised her hand and boarded the train without another glance. She didn't want to go. Jonne didn't want to go this time, either. His best friend is having a birthday party, but the damn agreement she has with Torben stipulates that the children have to go to Berlin every fortnight. There they sit in a small room in a semifurnished apartment and are largely left to their own devices. Torben calls this freedom.

Recently he's been leading a rather esoteric life, in which herbs and fumigation appear to play a significant role. When the children come back to Leipzig it's not just their clothes and hair that stink of burnt wood, resin, and herbs, but their bags, hairbrushes, schoolbooks, and cuddly toys too. She immediately washes anything that can be washed, including the children.

In the early days Ada wanted to go straight back to Berlin. Her anger only dissipated when she made friends in her new class, and it wasn't long before she refused to spend every other weekend with Torben in Berlin. Her old friendships in the capital were soon no more, and she found it unbearable to sleep in the same room as Jonne.

On a few occasions Jorinde gave in. She enjoyed watching the children settle calmly and contentedly into the dependable routine that she and Malika were creating. But then Torben brought in the Child Welfare Office and everything started again from scratch. Rushing home after school on Fridays, packing their things, driving to the station, and putting the children on a train taking them to a world without rules, fixed mealtimes, or their newly acquired friends. On Sunday evening another train spits them out again. For days Jorinde has to battle the effects of what happens in between, and by the time things have stabilized again, Ada and Jonne are back on a train.

She grates ginger into the mortar, adds garlic, chili, turmeric, and pepper, and grinds everything down with the pestle. Then she fries some onions, stirs the paste into the hot oil, pours in coconut milk, and adds the cut-up chicken.

Lilli loves meat. All meat. She even devours liver with relish.

The big children envy Lilli. She never has to go away. Her father silently pays money and doesn't interfere. When she's old enough, he'll be there for her.

At supper Lilli is sitting next to Malika.

Jorinde's phone beeps. The rule for Ada and Jonne is: no mobile phones at the table. The discussions they have about this are hard work, especially as Jorinde fails to stick to the rule herself. She glances at Malika, then takes the phone from her trouser pocket and reads: Am already here. Victor's Residenz-Hotel. Will you come soon? Love, Albrecht.

She knows him from the filming after Lilli was born. He played the part of Hugo von Hoffmansthal, while she was Elsa Bruckmann, wife of the publisher Hugo Bruckmann, salon hostess and, later, Hitler supporter.

The film wasn't a success, but fortunately the critics pounced on the mediocre screenplay. Jorinde's portrayal of Elsa Bruckmann, on the other hand, met with unanimous praise. If anything saved this film, it was her. She was the only reason to watch it, the journalists said. Their acclaim pushed her to the next level, where the roles became more interesting.

Since working together Albrecht and she have been bonded

by a friendship to which they added a physical relationship. Something Malika wouldn't understand.

Yup, on my way, she types, then presses send.

Meanwhile Lilli has pushed her vegetables to the edge of the plate and is shoveling down her meat. Each of her children is different. Ada is eccentric and highly intellectual, Jonne introverted and totally uninterested in school, and Lilli is simply joyful. With her giggly laugh, her love of music, and the concentration with which she puts away her food, she gives the impression that her entire existence is blessed with happiness. Nothing seems to weigh her down. She rarely cries, sleeps well, and takes any new thing completely in her stride. Jorinde is briefly tempted to lie down with Lilli and doze off beside her. But then comes another message from Albrecht.

Champagne on ice. Hurry!

I've got to go, she says to Malika. *Could you put Lilli to bed?*

Malika nods and reminds her for the umpteenth time that she won't be able to look after Lilli for the next few evenings.

Yes, I know, Jorinde says, then kisses them both good-bye.

It's not easy. When coordinating their schedules, they often need recourse to babysitters. Malika mainly teaches late afternoon. The state of the apartment and their differing ideas on how to bring up children occasionally lead to arguments too. But unlike Torben, Malika is prepared to discuss things. With her it's easy to reach a compromise, and Jorinde never feels cheated afterward.

Malika is the best as far as Lilli is concerned, and when she started to talk, she said *Mama* and *Mali* at about the same time.

Sometimes Malika keeps her distance. If Lilli calls for her too often, for example, or cuddles up to her too much, she'll gently push her away and say, *Go to Mama*. And with the arrival of each season she announces she's leaving the apartment. Jorinde took her seriously the first time and got a fright the second time too.

But Malika is still here.

In the taxi Jorinde takes out her pocket mirror and puts on some red lipstick. As far as she knows there's no man in her sister's life apart from Cold Eyes. They avoid the subject. Their few attempts to broach it have ended in Malika's silence.

She'll go with Bertram Weisshaupt to the cinema, a concert, a restaurant, or on a trip out of town. But the relationship appears to be asexual and unclear. Sometimes he won't be on the scene for weeks, and then they'll see each other every few days. He never comes into their apartment; he can't on account of his allergy to cat hair. And because Malika doesn't like his Doberman she won't go to his place, either.

The taxi stops outside the hotel.

Enjoy the night shift! the driver says with a wink. By the time she grasps what he means, he's long gone.

Albrecht is waiting in the foyer. He's standing in the middle of the room, smiling at her. She likes his self-assurance. Insecure men don't interest her. They take a lift to the third floor without saying much. In the room he takes a rapid HIV test in front of her. In London, where he spends most of the year, these are available at every chemist's.

Jorinde declines. *With me there's nothing to test*, she says.

He frowns in disbelief. *It's been almost four months.*

Well, she says with a shrug, *you need to come more often, then.*

Albrecht strokes her cheek, then fills two glasses with champagne, and glugs his back immediately.

His test is negative.

They get undressed, each with their gaze fixed on the other. Halfway down his body she finds the visible confirmation that he wants her.

She's getting older; the tattoos on her upper arms and back, which she's regretted over and over again, are fading and losing their shape. Stretch marks spread across her bottom and thighs, but this doesn't seem to bother Albrecht. He satisfies her more than any man has been able to in the past. And she doesn't love him. She'll only confide her most secret desires to a man she doesn't love.

*

The following morning Jorinde takes a taxi home. Her meetings with Albrecht alienate her from her usual environment and so she behaves like a stranger. She is chauffeured around and views the city through the eyes of a traveler.

Malika and Lilli aren't there.

This gives her a bit of time to herself. The reverse transformation is an energy-sapping metamorphosis—as if a butterfly were being forced back into the cocoon, to emerge again in paler colors.

Jorinde suspects that Malika has never experienced such divisions. She would have found it easier to be a mother. But life doesn't play out like that.

Jorinde is still in the shower when Lilli skips into the bathroom and puts the children's toilet trainer onto the toilet seat. She wrestles her tights down, pushes the step stool from the sink to the toilet, and climbs onto it.

Ada and Jonne were never so independent at this age.

Everything all right in there? Malika calls out.

Yes, Jorinde says, *she's on the toilet.*

Where have you two been? she asks after drying herself and getting dressed.

At the playground. And where were you, may I ask? I didn't realize you were going to be away for the night.

Malika! I'm still young. Sometimes I need—

Watch it! Malika says.

Lilli comes running into the kitchen. She's dragging the violin case behind her and drops it by Malika's feet.

You've got your next pupil, Jorinde says, as her sister checks to see whether the instrument is damaged and directs some strict words at Lilli. *You have to be careful. That's my violin, Lilli. Not yours. Mine.*

Mine, Lilli repeats.

She can't just drag a twenty-thousand-euro violin across the floor, Malika says, shaking her head.

Jorinde's ears prick up.

Where did you get that from? she says.

My violin?

No, the twenty thousand.

Mama and Papa gave me fifteen thousand at the time, she says reluctantly.

The look on her face betrays her guilty conscience. Jorinde never got a sum of money like that. What do her parents think? That all actors are rich? The fancy clothes she's wearing in the magazine photographs weren't hers. The price for renting a decent evening gown is three hundred euros. Add to that the jewelry, makeup, hairdresser, and taxi, and a gala evening will set her back five hundred euros. And she has to be seen. She needs to maintain existing contacts and forge new ones—all this with three children. The most successful of her fellow actresses either have no children or one at most.

Lilli has wrapped herself around her leg. They call it the koala game. Jorinde has to wander around the apartment with her because baby koalas hang on to their mothers like that. They saw it in the zoo. She goes once around the table before gently shaking Lilli off.

By the way, Malika says, *Viktoria rang earlier.*

And?

Next month Helmut's playing with the orchestra for the very last time. He'd like us to be there for his farewell concert. You, too.

Jorinde shakes her head.

Malika says the city's too small to be able to avoid each other entirely, but that's not true. Their paths don't cross and she has no intention of changing this.

Jorinde hasn't spoken to her father since the day he refused to give security for their apartment. More than two years have passed since. Not doing something for two years lasts longer than doing it for that time. Einstein had a better explanation, but even she knows that time isn't a constant variable.

The children, on the other hand, see their grandparents regularly and enjoy doing so. That contact is particularly important for Ada. Sometimes Malika brings Lilli along, too.

When he leaves the orchestra, Helmut intends to become politically engaged. Jorinde thinks she knows which direction that will be in. All they need now is for him to run for office and have his face appear on posters with his name printed underneath. Then Torben would let everybody know whose daughter she is. Even when she was playing Elsa Bruckmann he sneeringly told people how perfectly apt the role was for her: *The daughter of a Nazi playing a supporter of Adolf Hitler.*

Sometimes she feels ashamed that she ever got together with Torben.

And sometimes she can't remember what exactly Helmut has to apologize to her for. Viewed soberly it was just his tone that was wrong. Maybe the only reason she's not talking to him is that she hasn't spoken to him for too long.

Lilli keeps trying to get into Malika's room.

Lilli, too, she whines. Jorinde clamps the child under her arm and carries her into her own room. They romp around on the bed for a while, but as soon as Jorinde's attention wavers, Lilli scampers into the hallway and makes for Malika's bedroom. Jorinde puts on a coat, scoops Lilli up, and leaves the apartment.

Lilli loves the freight bicycle. She sits in the box at the front, bedded on soft furs, a cushion at her back, and her toy meerkat in her arm.

The tangy fragrance of ramsons wafts over from the Rosental. They've often been to the woods before the plants blossom and picked the young leaves, after which they've spent days preparing recipes using wild garlic. Malika can't get enough of them.

They do a circuit of the large park in the Rosental before turning into the woods. Jorinde likes being close to the water. They pass the Weisse Elster and Parthe Rivers, and then keep to the path that runs along the Neue Luppe. At the artificial lake they lock up the bike and get on the park train, on a narrow-gauge track that in the days of the GDR was known as the Pioneers' Railway. The locomotive puffs out steam and they ride around the lake. Pedaloes glide across the water like giant swans, and it strikes Jorinde that when wonder ends, death must be close.

*

On Sunday the train from Berlin arrives forty minutes late.

Jonne gets out first.

Where's Ada? she asks anxiously.

She sat somewhere else.

Then she sees her daughter standing farther down the platform. Ada puts her rucksack over her shoulder and approaches her very slowly. *Papa's an arse*, she says instead of a greeting. She leans her head on Jorinde's chest and lets her mother hug her.

Her scruffiness has reached a new height. On her feet are

white Nike socks and Adidas slides, and she wears baggy sweat-pants on her thin legs. Before Jorinde can ask any questions Ada pulls her headphones over her ears and keeps on going.

What happened? she asks Jonne, who walks beside her.

Hanging his head, he says, *We're not to see Grosspapa and Grossmama anymore.*

She stops. *He can't decide that.*

He says he can.

Why?

Because Grosspapa told Ada she should cross the street if she sees a group of Arabs coming toward her.

Jorinde groans.

I'm sorry, she says. *I'll sort it out.*

✳

On the tram Ada takes off her headphones and asks abruptly, *Is it up to Papa if I see Grosspapa?*

No, Jorinde replies. *You have every right to visit your grandparents.*

Visibly satisfied, Ada goes straight back to her music. Jorinde catches a few bars. If she's not mistaken its Bach's *Cello Suite No. 1.* Ada is a mystery.

Back home Malika is waiting impatiently. She's dressed and made up for a chamber concert that evening in some small local town.

Is that Herr Weisshaupt outside? Jorinde says, getting ready to catch Lilli, who's running at full pelt toward her, without the slightest doubt, it seems, that she'll land safely in her mother's arms. The energy in her approach is enough for them to spin around a few times.

Yes, he's driving me there, Malika says.

Then she turns to Ada and Jonne and asks about their weekend.

I'm not going anymore, Ada says.

Then I'm not going either, Jonne adds.

Malika stops midstep and glances at Jorinde, her eyebrows raised. Jorinde waves a hand dismissively. *You've got to go, we'll talk about it tomorrow.*

Malika nods. Lilli runs behind her into the stairwell and shouts as loudly as she can: *Bye-eee!*

*

The following morning, when the children have left the apartment, Jorinde makes some tea and has breakfast in peace. Her sister is still asleep. She got back late, after midnight. Jorinde was lying awake, heard the door close, and wondered how Malika and Cold Eyes said good-bye.

Soon after, Malika pokes her head around the door to mumble *Good morning!* and trudges off to the bathroom, and then the telephone rings for the first time. It's her agent. Two job offers have come in. One of them is interesting: a biopic of the Swedish painter Hilma af Klint. The upside—it's the lead role; the downside—nobody's heard of Hilma af Klint.

No sooner has she put the phone down than it rings again.

This time it's the man from the Child Welfare Office. Torben wants a change in his visitation rights. It's suggested that they meet to discuss this a fortnight from today.

I can't, Jorinde says. *I've got an audition for a film.*

How about the following week, then? Wednesday morning?

She checks her diary. *Sorry, I'm filming in Hamburg for two days.*

She can hear him clear his throat. *Frau Amsinck, if you're going to place your own interests above those of your children—*

The father of my children doesn't pay any child support. I have to work to earn money.

That may well be, but your children's father is making the time. He tells me he could come to any appointment.

Jorinde exhales to control her mounting anger. *Are there any slots available this week? Of course I'd like to get this sorted out as quickly as possible.*

She hears the rustling of paper, then he says, *Someone's canceled tomorrow morning.*

Perfect! she replies. *Will you call my ex-husband?*

When he hangs up, she feels sick.

*

In the night Lilli starts crying. She feels hot to the touch. Jorinde's first thought is of her appointment. Torben will come. If she blows him off, that will be another black mark against her. The thermometer reads 102.2. She creeps into the kitchen and looks at their joint planner. Malika has a dentist's appointment, so that rules her out. She could ask Vicky, but doesn't want to. Going back into Lilli's room with a damp flannel, she cools her brow and lies next to her. It's almost half past one.

At around three o'clock she gives her daughter some syrup to lower her temperature and half an hour later they're both asleep. The alarm goes off at ten to six.

She has to call Jonne three times before he gets up. *Who's taking me to my guitar lesson today, you or Malika?* he says, taking a sip of his hot chocolate. Jorinde looks at her daughter.

Not me! Ada says. *Can't he go on his own? It's two stops, Mama, then five minutes' walk.*

Jorinde looks at Jonne. *Could you manage that?*

I could, he says with his mouth full. *But I don't want to.*

She sits beside him and strokes his head. Only then is her attention caught by Ada's hoodie—emblazoned across the chest are the words: THERE'S A FUCKIN' IDIOT STARING AT ME. Ada grins and shows Jorinde the back: STILL STARING AT ME.

Where did you get that? she asks.

From Papa.

She kisses the children good-bye and says *I love you very much* to each of them in turn. They've had this little ritual ever since the daughter of a friend of hers was hit by a lorry on the way to school and killed. They'd been having a blazing row and the last words the mother said to her child were: *Get out, now!*

At seven o'clock Jorinde's sitting at the table with a strong black coffee, wondering whether Ada, Jonne, and Lilli will survive their childhood more or less unscathed. Whether they'll turn into strong adults. The degree of havoc all grown-ups wreak in this world is relative to how damaged they were as children.

Then she thinks of Malika. How angry her sister was as a child, fractious but also quiet. And how the only man she ever loved cheated on her and left. Malika still won't talk about it. Their parents found her by the door to his workshop and took her to the clinic. Only the apathy she fell into every morning and evening after taking her medicine released her from Götz.

The Cipramil is still in the lockable bathroom cabinet, and maybe it's the high serotonin level that makes Malika's life at all possible.

Υ

Torben sneers at her. There's an unnerving confidence in his face that manifests itself as a grin. He's got time. Every few weeks he comes up with a new demand she has to grapple with, and each time she hates him more.

On the table in the meeting room are a water bottle and two glasses. Torben helps himself. He finishes it in one gulp, puts the glass down forcefully, and starts whistling quietly to himself. Lilli looks at him with curiosity, cuddling up close to Jorinde with her thumb in her mouth.

We're here today at the father's request, says Herr Kölmel, the counselor for clients whose surname begin with A. *The children in question are Ada and Jonne Amsinck.* He takes out his pen, gets a sheet of paper ready, and gives Torben a nod of encouragement. *Go ahead, please, Herr Amsinck.*

What Jorinde then hears sounds as if it's been worked out by a lawyer; it contains responses to every possible objection. He's come well prepared.

The reasoning is simple. He and his new partner are expecting a child, and they want Ada and Jonne to live full-time with them. Unlike Jorinde, he can offer the children a stable family structure: father, mother, children, and a new sibling. Unlike Jorinde's father, his parents wouldn't pollute the children with right-wing propaganda. She can see the delight in his eyes as he paints a picture of her father, which resembles Helmut about as much as the real Torben does the actor sitting opposite her. He doesn't want his children to see this man again.

She's about to object when Herr Kölmel intervenes: *We insist on peaceful communication here, Frau Amsinck, which means we allow everybody to finish what they have to say.*

I've got to get rid of that name, she thinks, as Torben continues and Herr Kölmel is again busy writing.

Unlike Jorinde, he's faithful and reliable. He would like to remind her that the girl on her lap was the product of an affair. Jorinde probably cheated on him several times, he says, and he can't imagine that his ex-wife's lifestyle has changed that much. For two years he's reluctantly contented himself with being a weekend papa, but it's not enough.

Lilly wriggles from her arms. She toddles back and forth and takes a hole punch from the table. *It's fine*, Herr Kölmel says.

The thoughts are rattling around Jorinde's head. Suddenly Torben's threat makes sense. When she applied for child support because he wasn't paying, he rang her. *The state's claiming all the fucking money back from me,* he screamed. *I keep getting letters from the welfare office!*

They're your children too, she replied. *You ought to be happy that the state's taking over your responsibilities.*

He laughed scornfully and hung up. A few minutes later he called again and said, very calmly, *You'll be sorry you said that.*

Herr Kölmel gives her an inquiring look. *Frau Amsinck,* he says in the tone of a therapist, *can you imagine the children living with Herr Amsinck permanently?*

As he waits for an answer he shows Lilli how the hole punch works. She enthusiastically begins making holes in the cover of a brochure. Clearing her throat, Jorinde says, *Herr Amsinck doesn't even pay child support for the children. I wonder how he imagines it would work?*

Torben smiles. *That wouldn't be necessary anymore,* he says. *We could happily set the outstanding child support payments against what my ex-wife has to pay me.*

She fixes him with a stare. *Have you asked the children what they want? They don't want to live with you. They don't want to go to Berlin anymore.*

He leans back and crosses his arms. *So your sister's a substitute for their father, is she?*

Herr Kölmel stops writing and gestures with his hands for them to calm down. *The only consideration here is the children's welfare.*

The children are fine, Jorinde says. *I reject Herr Amsinck's proposal.*

For a moment she fancies she can see relief in Herr Kölmel's eyes. If he's on her side, then he's made a damn good show of hiding it.

Torben's face twitches. *See you in court, then.* She senses his anger. A few more choice words and the fine thread of her ex-husband's patience will snap. Herr Kölmel wouldn't like Torben unchained.

Lilli has clearly done enough punching. She looks to see what else there is of interest on Herr Kölmel's table and climbs back onto Jorinde's lap with a Tipp-Ex correction tape mouse. Her forehead is hot again and her eyes are gleaming feverishly.

Let's call it a day, Jorinde says. *My daughter's not well.*

She says good-bye with Lilli in her arms. Torben merely nods at her.

This here, he says, *is unfinished business!*

Malika is waiting outside. She's borrowed the car from Cold Eyes and has even remembered a child seat. Her right cheek is swollen. *One tooth down,* she mumbles with a shrug.

Jorinde puts Lilli into the car and belts her up. *He's taking me to court,* she says flatly. *I don't know if I can cope with that.*

As ever, Malika's embrace feels limp, as if she's trying to avoid genuine contact. But her words contradict this impression. *You don't have to go through this alone,* she says. *I'm here for you.*

Without saying another word she navigates the car through the heavy traffic. At the next set of lights Jorinde turns to Lilli. Her dark locks are sticking to her forehead and her eyes are half closed. More than one person has mistaken her for Malika's daughter, and it's always been Malika who has put them right.

Back home they all lie in Malika's bed, Lilli asleep between them. Jorinde looks at her sister, who has taken a painkiller and seems to be sleeping, too.

She can imagine living like this for a long time.

✳ ✳ ✳

It's the Resurrection Symphony. Mahler's second.

Helmut is pleased about this. His last appearance on the big stage. Five whole movements. One and a half hours of grandiose music.

Extraordinarily the children didn't protest. Ada demanded money to buy a dress for the occasion, and Jonne said he might become a musician, too, one day. He ignored her argument that he'd have to practice.

Jorinde even briefly considered bringing Lilli. *She's two years old*, Malika said, rolling her eyes. *Why on earth would you take her to listen to a Mahler symphony?*

Of course they have the best seats in the middle of the gallery. When the Allegro—the funeral rites—begins, Vicky fleetingly takes Jorinde's hand. In the fifth movement, the Resurrection, she wipes a few tears from the corners of her eyes.

Jorinde has never liked Mahler. Too bombastic, too march-like, too many instruments. Listening to it overwhelms and exhausts her. She's only here because of her father.

At the end of the concert, when the applause gradually dies down, the conductor says a few words. He asks the cellist Helmut Noth to stand, then he thanks an outstanding musician and ever-reliable member of the orchestra for his many years of loyal service and urges the audience to give him another round of applause. Then a girl appears on the stage with a bunch of flowers and gives it to Helmut. Less than a minute later most of the concertgoers get up from their seats and stream toward the exits.

That was it.

*

They're waiting for him at home with sekt and hors d'oeuvres. They raise a toast, then Vicky tells all the others to go and she shuts the door.

His hands are in his trouser pockets, his feet apart. As ever, his head is slightly bowed, but his eyes are fixed on her.

Jorinde slowly approaches him.

About the Author

DANIELA KRIEN was born in 1975 in Mecklenburg-Vorpommern in the then GDR. Her first novel, *Someday We'll Tell Each Other Everything*, was published in English in 2013 (MacLehose Press) and in fourteen other languages. For a subsequent volume of short stories, *Muldental*, she was awarded the Nicolas Born Prize. She lives in Leipzig with her two daughters.

About the Translator

JAMIE BULLOCH is the translator of novels by Timur Vermes, Steven Uhly, Martin Suter, Arno Geiger, and Roland Schimmelpfennig, and of crime fiction by Romy Hausmann, Oliver Bottini, and Peter Beck. For his translation of Birgit Vanderbeke's *The Mussel Feast*, he was the winner of the Schlegel-Tieck Prize.

A Note from the Translator

I'm often asked what the most difficult thing was to translate in a particular text. Surprisingly, it's rarely those long compound nouns that German can throw together at will, or the meandering sentences intricately held together with grammatical sophistication, but rather the short, seemingly simple words, phrases, or constructions that are usually among the most common in the language.

As in Daniela Krien's debut novel, *Someday We'll Tell Each Other Everything*, here too the author's style—often in striking contrast to the intensity of emotion it conveys—is understated, economical, almost to the point of simplicity. So far, so good, one might think; after all, English is a language well-suited to straightforward prose. And indeed, individually the sentences posed few problems. But very soon an unwelcome pattern emerged. In my translation, a large proportion of the sentences were ending up with a rigid subject, verb, object structure; far too many for comfort were beginning with "she." The narrative was in danger of sounding like a seven-year-old's report of their summer holiday.

This is not the case in the original. Like all inflected languages, German enjoys a large degree of flexibility in its word order, one feature of which is that the subject does not need to precede the verb. On the contrary, it is not uncommon to find the object opening the clause. And thus a succession of relatively simple German sentences can exhibit far greater diversity and elegance than their direct English equivalents.

One strategy I adopted to break the monotony was to use a character's name with greater regularity than in the original. While this reduced the number of sentences starting with "she," it did little to alter the overall cadence of the prose. Another tactic was to move a different part of speech, usually an adverb, to the beginning of a clause. Here I had to be careful, however, to avoid the language sounding stilted and artificial. The third ploy was to disrupt the original sentence structure, sometimes turning one sentence into two, elsewhere joining two into one. This allowed a more natural rhythm to emerge, which provided for syntactical variety while reflecting the style of the German original.

Within the art of literary translation, reference is frequently made to capturing the "voice" of a text. This goal is crucial to the success of rendering a novel into another language, which no amount of accurate line work can make up for. And as should be apparent from the above, the translator needs to think boldly and creatively, often having to make what might at first appear quite considerable changes in order to remain faithful to the spirit and melody of the original.

—Jamie Bulloch

Here ends Daniela Krien's
Love in Case of Emergency.

The first edition of this book was printed and
bound at LSC Communications in
Harrisonburg, Virginia, March 2021.

A NOTE ON THE TYPE

The text of this novel was set in Fairfield, a typeface
created by Czech-American engraver and designer
Rudolph Ruzicka (1883–1978). Ruzicka made his mark
as a design consultant for the Mergenthaler Linotype
Company for fifty years. He approached typeface design
with the philosophy that "type is made to be read, and
that implies a reader." Fairfield, one of Ruzicka's trade-
mark typefaces, was first designed for Linotype in 1940.
With its straight, unbracketed serifs and stark contrast
between thin and thick strokes, Fairfield is a contempo-
rary type with old-fashioned flair. It is decidedly elegant
and easy on the eyes.

HARPERVIA

An imprint dedicated to publishing international voices,
offering readers a chance to encounter other lives and other
points of view via the language of the imagination.